DEADLY ERRAND

Other Avalon Books by Lee Anderson

FAMILY SECRETS
LOVE'S TENDER CHALLENGE
THE RHINESTONE MONKEY

Deadly Errand

LEE ANDERSON

AVALON BOOKS
THOMAS BOUREGY AND COMPANY, INC.
401 LAFAYETTE STREET
NEW YORK, NEW YORK 10003

JY CH MC MB

PRINTED IN THE UNITED STATES OF AMERICA
BY HADDON CRAFTSMEN, SCRANTON, PENNSYLVANIA

To Don, of course

Chapter One

Peggy Hale made a face at the mouthpiece of the phone in her hand. Mr. Tyler could be a very verbose man. Right now he was giving her an endless list of reasons why the Calloway file had to be delivered—by her—to his cabin on Mt. Laguna that evening. Being her boss, Mr. Tyler could also be very persuasive.

His partner in the Tyler Advertising Agency, Randall Barker, had been at the cabin for two days enjoying a little rest and relaxation. Randall was planning to leave the cabin at seven the next morning to keep an eleven o'clock appointment with the people at Calloway Enterprises at their Los Angeles office. Mr. Tyler had intended to take the file up to him, but he was marooned in San Francisco because of the weather. There was no phone at the cabin, so he couldn't let Randall know he couldn't make it. "You know how important the Calloway account is to us, Peggy. The file is locked in an attaché case in the safe. I know I can trust you."

Peggy inhaled deeply, knowing that others could always count on her to be a sucker for such an appeal. "I understand, Mr. Tyler. I'll take the

1

file up to Randall." Mr. Tyler was in a spot and she was more than willing to help him out, but her own life was too often complicated by her inability to say no to anyone needing her help. In November darkness came early; it was already after four, and she wasn't thrilled by the thought of driving alone at night. Also, storm clouds had been gathering all day and it was sure to start raining soon. The prospect of driving home in the rain was hardly cheering either.

"Look, Peggy," Mr. Tyler said in his gravelly voice, "I know it's a long drive up there, but you shouldn't run into much traffic. If Randall isn't there when you arrive, leave the attaché case just inside the door. He has my keys, so if he has to go out for some reason, he'll leave the door unlocked. I told him I'd be there by seven at the very latest. He said he'd try to wait for me. You won't have any trouble making it by seven if you leave right now."

She certainly wouldn't plan on it. "I know I'll be all right, Mr. Tyler," she lied.

"We'll make it up to you. I'd asked my wife to run it up, but she had back-to-back appointments this afternoon. I don't know what they are. She does her own thing, you know. She left here early this morning."

From what Peggy knew, Jennifer Tyler was indeed a woman who did "her own thing," but Peggy had gotten her information from the office grapevine, which was not known for its adherence to the facts. After Mr. Tyler refreshed her memory with directions to his cabin, she ended the conversation at the first opening she could find in his monologue.

Lillian Frye, Mr. Tyler's secretary, was at the big safe when Peggy arrived. She gave the prim woman a brief report of her call from Mr. Tyler. With just a look, Lillian could make people feel they should explain their actions. Peggy lifted the attaché case from the safe and groaned. "Good grief, this is heavy!" She placed it on the floor while she regained her breath. Then she took her car keys from her shoulder bag and picked up the attaché case again. "I'd better get going. Good night, Lillian. Have a nice weekend."

Lillian scowled and followed Peggy to the door. "I wondered what was in that case. He put it in there the night before he left for San Francisco. I can't imagine why he'd put the Calloway file in the safe. You know, Peggy, you shouldn't have been so quick to say you'd go up there. A big storm is about to break. You don't have to do this to make points with the boss. He already thinks you're heaven's gift to the Tyler Advertising Agency." Lillian's tone carried the touch of scorn everyone at Tyler Advertising knew so well.

"Really, Lillian, it's no big thing. I'll go home, change my clothes, and be on my way." Peggy often found it difficult not to respond sharply to Lillian's pointed remarks. But since she respected

Lillian's age and her tenure with Tyler Advertising and wished to maintain peace in the workplace, Peggy bit her tongue a lot and ignored Lillian when she could. According to the grapevine, Lillian had worked for the Tyler family since the beginning of time, and she had made a career of disapproving of everyone's actions.

Peggy loved her job as general manager of the Tyler Advertising Agency. Layout work was her specialty, but she had the responsibility of coordinating the work of copywriters, artists, photographers, and everyone else whose efforts produced ad copy that pleased their clients. She also spent time with clients trying to figure out ways to transfer their ideas to print advertising copy.

She felt she had little to complain about in her life that day, except that it would be dark when she arrived at the remote cabin in the mountains. She had been there only once before, and she would probably have to drive the sixty or more miles back to the city in the rain. People did it all the time, she told herself. Knowing that didn't help much.

The traffic slowed to a crawl and then stopped just before she reached the turnoff for her apartment building. Long lines of cars sat motionless, probably because of an accident up ahead. Peggy sat and waited, since she had no choice. When the car ahead of her finally inched forward, she glanced at her watch: five o'clock. She could still make the cabin at Mt. Laguna by seven, she told herself, providing the traffic didn't linger too much longer.

At five-twenty she arrived at her apartment. She changed from high heels to jogging shoes, grabbed an umbrella, and dashed out the door. It was a quarter to six when she turned onto Highway 8 and headed east. She doubted she'd get to the cabin by seven, but she wouldn't be much later, barring anything unforeseen. She shuddered at that thought.

The black menacing clouds continued to blend and move and threaten as she drove through El Cajon Valley toward the mountains. Palm fronds lashed against one another angrily. After she passed the turnoff for the town of Alpine, the traffic thinned down to a trickle, and somehow that made her more apprehensive than she had been in the heavier commuter traffic. By the time she turned onto Sunrise Highway, which would take her to the section of Mt. Laguna where many vacation cabins were scattered among the trees, she had the sinking feeling she might not find Mr. Tyler's cabin. In the gloomy darkness, one cabin set back among the pines looked pretty much like all the others spread so sparsely about.

None too soon, she spotted a familiar corner. A house had burned to the ground some time ago, but the chimney still stood defiantly. Turning onto the dirt road, she eased her car along to the last cabin, beside which sat Randall's red sports car. She let out a long sigh of relief, though her heart sank a little when she noticed the cabin was dark. Maybe Randall had fallen asleep on the couch, she told herself hopefully. She wanted Randall to be there. It was spooky enough beneath the dark, cloudy sky. The thought of opening the door to that dark cabin, even for just a minute, tightened her chest and sent shivers racing through her.

She picked up her shoulder bag and the attaché case and got out of the car, looking around for a sign of life. She told herself she was foolish to feel apprehensive. In the distance a dog howled, giving her little comfort. Wind whistled through the thick stand of evergreen trees around her as she made her way over a long crushed-rock path leading to the cabin steps.

She stepped onto the small porch and rapped loudly on the door. There was no answer. She rapped three more times, making enough noise to wake the dead, she thought. She called Randall's name several times, but only that lone dog in the distance answered. She turned the knob of the front door. It was locked. "Marvelous," she said sarcastically. Randall had probably locked the door from habit when he left.

Peggy was definitely not at her most courageous in strange surroundings in the dark. Mustering all the bravado she could, she stepped off the porch and walked cautiously around to the back of the cabin. After knocking endlessly on the back door and receiving no answer to her repeated shouts, she tried the door. It, too, was locked. "What now?" she asked the door. There was no mailbox. She couldn't just leave the attaché case, with the important papers inside, on the open porch with the imminent threat of rain. No windows were open. The wind continued to whistle through the trees, and she hunched her shoulders against the cold air. Then it began to sprinkle.

Shivering, she walked over to Randall's car. If it was unlocked, she could place the attaché case inside with a note and lock the car. But all the doors were efficiently locked and the windows were closed. Hoping for a new idea to hit her, she looked around. A man was standing by an open door of her car. She drew in a sharp breath and yelled at him, "Hey! What are you doing to my car?"

He whipped around. Instantly there was a cracking sound and something whizzed by her. For a moment she stood paralyzed, staring at the man, who was stretching out an arm in her direction. Pushing panic aside, she realized the man had shot at her. Faster than she'd have thought possible, she leaped behind the house as another shot rang through the air. She turned and raced into the woods just as the rain began in earnest.

She had no idea how far she ran. Finally she found herself gasping for air while her heart raced and she started to get a stitch in her side. Without a choice, she slowed a bit, then fell against a tree. While making a supreme effort to get her breath, she listened for the sound of someone coming after her. For a moment, only the heavy downpour of rain crashing through the trees broke the silence. Then she heard a twig snap. She caught her breath. She heard footsteps in the pine needles just as a hand fell on her shoulder. Her heart stopped. She leaped away and opened her mouth, but the scream stuck in her throat. Valiantly she kept swinging the attaché case at the form before her, trying to hit it, but the man kept ducking. "Hey, wait a minute," he said with a laugh.

"Why? So you can take another shot at me at close range?" she yelled. She took one more swing at him with the case, then turned and ran.

But she couldn't run as fast as she'd have liked. The undergrowth was thick and she was still winded. The man came after her and caught her. Before she could stop him, he pinned her arms to her side and pushed her against a tree. She continued to struggle. "Now wait a minute, lady," he said. "I didn't shoot at you. I'm one of the good guys."

She twisted and turned and kicked, making a monumental effort to get away from him. "I have no reason to believe that!" she yelled.

"Look, hold still, will you? My cabin is right over there. See the light? Come with me and you'll see I don't have a gun. I heard shots, and I came out to see what was going on."

"I don't know that!" she yelled again, then gave up the futile struggle. She still hadn't recovered her breath, and her heart continued to race at a breakneck speed.

"I know you don't, but I can prove I don't have a gun. Come back to my cabin."

"No. I don't know you." In the heavy rain, the man's face was a blur.

"What do you plan to do, run through the trees in the rain all night?" He took in an exasperated breath. "Look, my name is Nickolas T. Donovan, Jr. My family are nice people who live in La Mesa. I live in San Diego. I spent four years in the Marines, then went to college and earned an engineering degree, and now I work for TLM Corporation. I'm cold and wet and probably on the verge of pneumonia. Now that you know the story of my life, will you come to my cabin so we can get out of this downpour?"

Reluctantly she let him lead her to his cabin, since she didn't know what else to do. She was hopelessly lost, she was scared to death, she was drenched, and she wanted to believe it was all a bad dream. When they reached the cabin, he pushed open the door, reached inside, and turned on the porch light. "I want you to see I'm not concealing a gun." He spun around, holding his arms up in the air.

Along with a lightweight windbreaker, he wore jeans and a T-shirt that was soaked to his upper body. She looked him up and down.

"Okay," she said, squinting as she tried to see his face more clearly. "What are you doing up here, anyway?"

He waited for her to precede him into the cabin, but she stood her ground and let the rain wash over them while she waited for his answer. He shook his head. "Lady, you're something else. This cabin belongs to my folks. I came up here to be alone and have a nice relaxing few days and listen to my beard grow." He sneezed. "Thanks to you, I may now spend the first free time I've had in months in the hospital." He sneezed again.

"Bless you," she said as she stepped inside the cabin.

"Thanks a bunch. Go over to the fire," he ordered her as he left the room. Peggy walked over to the fire and stretched her cold wet hands to the warmth after she had laid the attaché case on the floor by her feet. The comfortably furnished large room had a natural-wood cathedral ceiling and paneled walls. She shivered, feeling a little skittish about being in this strange cabin with this strange man, but at the moment her alternatives seemed limited and no less hazardous, given the rain beating on the windowpanes. Nickolas came back into the room carrying two big mugs of steaming coffee. "I'll get you some dry clothes."

"No, thank you. I'll be fine. I'll just warm up a bit here by your fire, catch my breath, and be on my way." She rushed her words as she accepted the coffee. Drinking the steaming liquid helped. "Thank you. I wouldn't mind a towel to dry my face and hair, if you don't mind."

His smile, although quite nice, didn't calm her. He had changed to a dry T-shirt and combed his hair. Peggy tried not to think about what she looked like. "I'll show you to the bathroom," he said, adding, "I still think you should put on some dry clothes."

"I'll be fine, thank you," she assured him. In the small bathroom, she dried her face and hair before she looked in the mirror. Then she shuddered. Her face was totally devoid of makeup, and she'd seen mops that looked better than her hair. She replaced the towel on the rack. Though her appearance had always been important to her, she did not waste time repairing the damage. What was more important at the moment was the attaché case she had left on the floor by the fireplace. But when she returned to the big room, she found the case right where she'd left it.

Nickolas sat in one of the deep chairs in front of the fire. He sipped his coffee and watched her over the rim of his cup. When he placed his cup on the table beside him, he cocked his head to one side. "Now it's your turn to answer questions. Who are you? What are you doing running around in the woods in the rain, and why on earth was someone shooting at you?"

She cleared her throat and sat down across from him in the other chair by the fire. She probably did owe him some kind of an explanation, she decided, even though she wasn't sure what was going on. "My name is Peggy Sue Hale. I live in San Diego and work for Tyler Advertising. I brought this attaché case up to one of the partners, Randall Barker, but he's not at the Tyler cabin where he's supposed to be. Also, the front door is locked, though I was told it wouldn't be." She blinked, fighting back tears. "I have absolutely no idea why anyone would shoot at me." She closed her eyes tightly, trying to stop the flood. Then she looked at the man across from her. "Oh, Nickolas, I. . . ." She bit her lip.

He picked up his coffee mug and looked at it for a moment before telling her with a crooked grin, "My friends call me Nick."

That did it. He was laughing at her! She straightened her back, set her mug down with a thud, and wiped her eyes. "I'm sure they do. Is there a phone here?" There was no trace of friendliness in her voice.

"I'm afraid not. It's one of the charms of this place." He straightened up. "I know Mr. Tyler pretty well, but I don't know this Randall Barker. What's in that attaché case?"

Her composure regained, she glanced at the case on the floor and shrugged. "Just files for a client Randall is supposed to meet in the morning." She took a deep breath. Her heart had settled down somewhat and her lungs were handling the act of breathing quite well again. "I'm going back to that cabin. Randall may be there now. If I'm lucky, my assailant has left."

Nick frowned. "I don't think you should go back there." He stood up.

Peggy jumped up and picked up the attaché case. "I'll be all right." She adjusted her shoulder bag over one shoulder. She certainly didn't need this stranger telling her what she should do.

"Did you get a look at the man who shot at you?"

"He was too far away. I'm pretty sure he didn't follow me, though."

"Yeah, I am too. At least I didn't see anyone but you. Any chance it could be your Randall Barker?"

"Heavens, no. Randall has no reason to shoot me. Besides, the man wasn't built right. He was taller, I think, and his body was bulkier than Randall's."

"Do you really think you can find your way back through the woods?"

Peggy let out a long breath. "Probably not." She bit her lip. She hated to admit it. "Can you give me directions?"

"Come on, I'll drive you back to the Tyler cabin. But first we're going to check in at the sheriff's office. That guy could be waiting for you, you know."

She gulped. She hadn't thought of that. "I suppose so. I'm new at this. No one's ever shot at me before."

*   *   *

Two sheriff's deputies preceded them down the lane to the Tyler cabin, having cautioned Nick to wait at a distance for their signal. When one of the deputies waved his flashlight around, Nick drove to the dark cabin. The deputies had knocked on the front and back doors, called to Randall, and flashed their lights in the windows. They'd tried the doors and windows, but everything was locked. Randall's red car was still there. After talking to the deputies, Nick looked around. "It's a little strange that your Randall would go off on foot in the rain if he was expecting Mr. Tyler tonight," he said thoughtfully, looking off into the darkness.

Peggy looked around also, not feeling nearly as intimidated as she had earlier. "Well, he was supposed to leave the door unlocked if he left before Mr. Tyler arrived with the file."

Nick looked down at her. "What do you want to do?"

She took in her breath and let it out slowly, then squared her shoulders. "I think I'll go home." She couldn't think of anything else to do. "I'll leave a note on the door."

The deputy agreed that would be a good idea.

"If you want to leave the attaché case with me, I'll run it over here in the morning," Nick said.

Peggy couldn't consider that. She didn't know Nick Donovan. "Thanks, but I'll think of something." After she scribbled a note, Nick wedged it near the top of the door, out of the rain. She looked up at the sky. "I'm glad the rain is letting up." It was now little more than a healthy drizzle.

Nick looked up at the sky and nodded. "Look, Peggy, you can stay at my place, if you'd like. That way you can bring that attaché case over here early in the morning. Your Randall Barker is bound to be back by then. Or we can change your note and tell him to come to my place when he returns." He laughed lightly. "There's a second bedroom."

She stepped off the porch and started walking toward her car. She didn't miss the grin on the face of one of the deputies. "Thank you, Nick, but I have to get home." Her words were crisp.

Nick laughed. "I think you're nuts, but if you must, you must. I told you I'm one of the good guys."

"So you say." Again, her words were crisp.

One of the deputies asked if she had remembered any more about her assailant than she had told them at the station. She shook her head. "As I told you, I didn't really see the man. I haven't the foggiest idea who he might be. I know that not everyone loves me, but I can't believe I've ever incited anyone to shoot me. I don't know what he hoped to find in my glove compartment, but nothing's missing. If you don't need me for anything, I'll get going."

"That's it for now. Drive carefully, Miss

Hale," the younger deputy said as he held the door for her.

She looked at Nick. "Thanks for coming to my rescue." She got into her car and left. She started grumbling to herself as soon as she drove onto the freeway. It had been a shattering experience. She had every intention of telling every detail to both Randall and Mr. Tyler. This had certainly not been the way she'd have preferred to spend a Friday evening. As she drove down into the lights of El Cajon Valley, she decided she'd drop this whole thing into Mrs. Tyler's lap.

Chapter Two

It was almost eleven o'clock when Peggy arrived home. She was angry, tired, and starved, but she called Mr. Tyler's house immediately. No one answered, and she left her name and number on the answering machine. When she looked in the mirror, she couldn't believe what looked back at her. Her light-brown hair hung limply over her shoulders, showing no sign of the expertise she had developed with the blow dryer and curling iron. On her rain-washed face, her eyebrows were so pale as to appear nonexistent. Her new wool suit was probably ruined for life, and it hung so badly it made her look dumpy. Her shoes were covered with mud. She couldn't remember having ever looked worse.

After a long hot shower, she put on a warm fleecy robe and slippers and went into the kitchen. She made a sandwich while a pot of coffee perked. Sitting at the kitchen table, she relived the past few hours and tried to decide what she should do. When no brilliant idea came, she called the Tyler house again with the same result. She left her name again, this time with a message stressing urgency. She didn't mention the man

17

who had shot at her. *There's no sense upsetting Jennifer Tyler until I can talk to her,* Peggy told herself. If she couldn't reach Mrs. Tyler, she probably should forget the whole thing. *Under the circumstances, Mr. Tyler wouldn't expect me to go back, would he?* she asked herself.

Once in bed, Peggy relived the evening again. It occurred to her that Nick Donovan was quite an attractive man. His wet red-gold hair had glistened under the lamp by his chair. In memory she saw his fair skin, straight nose, and high forehead. His eyelashes were long and curled upward. She idly wondered what color his eyes were.

Why didn't I notice he was so handsome when I was with him? she wondered. *I was scared to death, that's why,* she reminded herself. As sleep started closing in, she guessed Nick was about four or five inches taller than she. That would make him about five ten or eleven. He appeared to be in his early thirties. She poked her pillow. What difference did it make what Nick Donovan looked like or how old he was? No doubt he thought she was a comical sight. She'd probably never see him again. With that disturbing thought, she drifted off to sleep.

Peggy had set the alarm for five, and it sounded off on time. She could not work up any enthusiasm for another trip to the cabin, but she had the feeling she should go. Maybe she should forget the whole thing, she told herself. How upset would everyone be? What would Randall do without the file? He couldn't go up to Calloway's office without the layouts. Maybe she should have left the attaché case with Nick Donovan. Maybe she should have waited for Randall to return. Maybe. . . . She threw back the covers and sat up. "Who knows?" she asked her slippers as she slid her feet into them.

She drank a cup of warmed-up coffee before she gave her hair a quick treatment with the curling iron. Still wondering what she should do, she pulled on a pair of jeans and a bulky warm sweater. She looked at the phone and bit her lip. Should she call again? On impulse she grabbed the phone and dialed the Tyler house, but again the answering machine took her call. She slammed the phone down. Before six in the morning, Jennifer Tyler wasn't likely to be a lot of help, anyway.

Peggy arrived at the Tyler cabin at seven-thirty, but she wasn't the first. Two sheriff's cars and two other cars sat near the cabin. Nick Donovan ran toward her and opened her car door. "There's a pretty good reason we couldn't get anyone to answer the door last night. Your boss, Mr. Tyler, was probably in there, but he may have been dead. I heard someone guess he's been dead about twelve hours."

Nick helped her out of the car while she tried

to absorb what he'd said. Just as she stood up, Jennifer Tyler walked around one of the sheriff's cars, stopped for a moment, and stared at Peggy. Then she shouted to a nearby sheriff's deputy, "There she is! She's the one I told you about. I know she came up here last night. She has to be the one who murdered my husband." She pointed directly at Peggy.

Peggy's mouth fell open, and for a panic-filled moment her mind went blank. She stared at Jennifer Tyler. Nick placed his hand on the small of her back and, somehow, she drew a little strength from it. "Mrs. Tyler, what are you talking about?" she asked.

"You came up here last night, I know you did. My husband called me about five o'clock yesterday and told me you were bringing some files up here to Randall. I called the office, and Lillian Frye assured me you were on your way and had the attaché case with you."

"I'm not denying I was here." She looked up at Nick. He picked up her hand and squeezed it. "This man and the sheriff's department know I was here, but I couldn't get any answer when I knocked on the door. The sheriff's deputies couldn't get an answer, either. Randall's car was here, but I couldn't find him." She took in a deep breath.

"But my husband was here apparently and you killed him." Jennifer burst into tears.

Peggy swallowed. "Mrs. Tyler, when Mr.

Tyler called me, he told me he was in San Francisco. A man was here and he shot at me." Her words ran together. Nick squeezed her hand again and led her toward the deputy and Mrs. Tyler. Nick told them everything he knew, from the sound of the shots to the moment he watched Peggy drive away. The deputy called a lieutenant over, and Nick and Peggy went over their stories again. She tried not to become hysterical, but it wasn't easy.

The lieutenant was thoughtful for a minute before he spoke. "I read the report about the man who shot at you, Miss Hale. Have you thought of anything else about him?"

She shook her head. "No. I told the deputies everything I could remember last night. I was over by that sports car, and it was beginning to rain and it was dark. I didn't hang around to get a good look at him, I assure you. I ran off through the woods. That's when I met Nick."

The lieutenant nodded. "Okay, for now. I'm going to want a more detailed statement from you, so stop at the station before you return to San Diego. Don't leave here until I say so." Just as the lieutenant finished speaking, a red car drove up and Randall Barker stepped out.

Randall walked over to Peggy and laid his hand on her arm. "Are you all right, Peggy?" he asked softly.

She pressed her lips together. "No, I'm not, Randall. I don't understand any of this. Mr.

Tyler told me you were staying here at the cabin, and he asked me to bring the Calloway file up to you. He told me he was in San Francisco."

Randall's wide brow creased as he looked around. "I left a message on his home answering machine the day before yesterday that I had called Calloway's office and they had postponed our appointment until next week. I said I'd be leaving here at dawn yesterday morning. It was too cold up here for me, and rain was in the forecast." He glanced over at Mrs. Tyler.

Peggy bit her lip. "I thought that was your car over there." She had to keep swallowing; her throat felt as though it was closing up.

Randall glanced at the car. "Obviously it's not. I just drove up here in my car." He turned away and went over to Mrs. Tyler. She started talking immediately and pointing at Peggy.

As Nick watched Randall, deep furrows lined his forehead. He spoke softly without looking away from Randall. "He's a cool one."

"It's part of his persona," Peggy said, turning her attention to Randall. "He never gets rattled. Mr. Tyler, on the other hand, was the temperamental and excitable one in the firm. When they had arguments, Mr. Tyler's voice was always the one that could be heard all over the office even with his office door closed." She looked up at Nick. "Have you learned anything that would make any sense of all this?" She noticed her hands weren't shaking quite as much. Either her nerves were settling down or she was becoming numb.

He clucked his tongue and looked down at her. "Not really. I was taking my morning run when I saw a sheriff's car turn up this road. Before I reached the turnoff for my cabin, the coroner's van passed me. I went home and thought about it for a while before I got into my car and came over. I had no idea what was going on, but I do know there are few people up in this area after summer ends. I thought I might be able to help someone."

Peggy looked up at him and smiled. "You're a nice man, Nick Donovan." She had the feeling she should be grateful she'd run into him.

"I told you I was one of the good guys." His eyes sparkled down at her.

She jabbed him gently in the ribs with her elbow and looked back at Randall and Mrs. Tyler. To her surprise she saw that Randall was staring back at her. He dropped his arm from Mrs. Tyler's shoulder and started walking toward her. Nick picked up her hand and squeezed it again. That helped. Speaking as though something had just occurred to him, Randall asked, "Peggy, do you have that file with you?"

She thought that was a dumb question. "Yes, of course. That's why I'm here now. Mr. Tyler told me you had that appointment in LA this morning with the Calloway firm."

Randall shook his head. "I wish he'd listened

to his answering machine. Let me see the attaché case."

Nick pulled the attaché case from the backseat of her car. Randall took it and laid it on the hood of Peggy's car. Mrs. Tyler moved closer and narrowly watched as he fumbled with the lock. Usually Mrs. Tyler's face was impeccably made up and she never allowed one bright red strand of hair to be out of place. Now her lipstick was all but missing, her eye makeup was smeared, and her hair was wildly tousled. Her appearance was understandable, of course, but a little shocking to see.

Randall went to his car and returned with a screwdriver. With some effort and Nick's help, he pried the case open. At the sight of what lay inside, Randall showed no expression, Mrs. Tyler bit her lip, and Peggy gasped in surprise. "You mean I've been running up and down this mountain with an attaché case full of newspapers?" she asked no one in particular.

Randall pulled four thick issues of the *San Diego Evening Tribune* from the attaché case. As Mrs. Tyler walked away, Peggy looked up at Nick and said, "No wonder that thing was so heavy."

Randall looked down at her. "You don't have a key to this, do you?"

"No!" Anger was building up in her. She resented the question. *Why am I involved in any of this?* she asked herself. She squeezed Nick's hand

and dropped it. The lieutenant was viewing the newspapers, and she felt he should be able to answer a couple of questions. "Lieutenant, who found Mr. Tyler's body?"

He looked surprised, probably because of the anger in her voice. "That deputy over there." She could tell it didn't thrill him to talk to her about it but she guessed her expression told him she wasn't going to let him stop there. He took a deep breath. "Mr. Kolby called us. He lives in that cabin over there." He pointed across the street at a small house that sat back from the road. "He's the only full-time resident on this street. He said several cars had gone back and forth to the Tyler place. He didn't think anyone was there, but there was a car parked in the driveway. We don't know who parked it there yet, but it's a rented car. Since the Tyler cabin sits back here at the end of the road and Mr. Kolby hadn't seen anyone around all day, the traffic concerned him. He did say that a man had been there for two days, earlier in the week, with a car just like the one parked in the driveway."

Peggy glanced at the red sports car similar to Randall's. "Did Mr. Kolby hear any gunshots?"

The lieutenant scowled at her. "Yes. At the time, he didn't think they were gunshots. Mr. Tyler has two bullet holes in him."

She shivered. "Did Mr. Kolby hear more than two shots?"

The lieutenant's expression said he'd had

enough of her questions. Exasperation came through his voice. "He's not sure how many shots he may have heard, but he thinks there were at least two at two different times." He pressed his lips together. "If your inquisition is over, Miss Hale, I have work to do. You might remember that you are the only one we know was here last night. The murdered man's wife feels quite sure you may have killed her husband." He turned and walked away.

Peggy ran after him. "One more thing, lieutenant. What time did the deputy find Mr. Tyler?"

He kept walking, but she kept up with him. He didn't look at her when he answered. "I'm not sure of the exact time, but I believe it was just after one o'clock this morning. When no one answered his knock, he tried the front door and found it unlocked. Inside he found Tyler on the floor in one of the bedrooms. Anything else, Miss Hale?"

She didn't miss the sarcasm, but chose to ignore it. "Well, the front door was locked when we were here," she persisted. "Did you call Mrs. Tyler right away?"

He stopped and turned to face her. "Look, Miss Hale, I'm not sure what you're after. We didn't find Mrs. Tyler's phone number until about four this morning. She came right up."

"I see." She was thoughtful for a moment. "I don't suppose I could look inside the cabin."

"You suppose correctly, Miss Hale."

"Lieutenant, did you call Randall Barker too?"

Now he was mad. "No, Miss Hale. When Mrs. Tyler arrived she told us she had called her husband's partner. She also told us she had called her husband's brother, who lives in LA. Now, if you have any more questions, please save them until later and let me get to work. At the moment you are the only suspect we have, and suspects don't usually ask the questions. You should be more concerned about your position."

Peggy waved her hand in the air. "That's ridiculous, lieutenant. I certainly didn't kill Mr. Tyler. I have trouble stepping on spiders."

His face relaxed a little, and he glanced at Peggy with a faint twinkle in his eyes. "Miss Hale, I believe I read somewhere that Jack the Ripper had a similar affliction." He turned and walked away.

She turned around and looked up at Nick. "You know, there's a lot here that just doesn't make sense."

He grinned down at her. "When you're not scared to death, you're . . . really something." His grin broadened.

"Thanks for not giving it a name. I've a lot more questions for that lieutenant."

"I bet you do. By the way, when you're dried out you look a whole lot better than you do soaking wet."

"Thanks a whole bunch." She scowled and

looked over toward Randall's car. "You know, I've been watching Mrs. Tyler and Randall. He's been holding her close and whispering in her ear. I never knew they were so friendly. Maybe he's just consoling her."

"Yeah, maybe."

"If that's it, he's doing a marvelous job."

"Yeah, I think I saw her stifling laughter a moment ago." Nick chuckled softly.

A man Peggy hadn't noticed before walked from the back of the house. "Nick, who's that man with the neck brace?"

"He got here just before you did. I heard someone say he was Mr. Tyler's brother."

"The lieutenant just mentioned that Mrs. Tyler had called her husband's brother. I didn't know Mr. Tyler had a brother."

At the sheriff's station, they had all given their statements and were waiting for them to be typed up for signatures. Mrs. Tyler, Randall, and Mr. Tyler's brother went outside. Peggy and Nick remained in the lieutenant's office.

"Lieutenant, I have a couple of questions I'd like to ask you," Peggy said, trying not to sound too pushy.

One eyebrow raised, he looked up at her. "Why doesn't that surprise me?" He leaned his long thin frame back in his chair. "Okay, Miss Hale, what is it now?"

She cleared her throat. "First I'd like to know

if I'm going to be arrested. No one has told me to call my attorney."

He laughed quietly and shook his head. "No, Miss Hale, for now I don't have any evidence against you. Knowing you were there last night is hardly enough." A smile continued to play around his lips. "There was a struggle in that cabin. The place is pretty messed up with over-turned furniture and lamps. Mr. Tyler has a broken leg and a lot of bruises on his face and body. We'll know more when we get the coroner's report, but right now it's hard to tell whether he died from the beating he took or from the gunshots. I'd say his opponent was probably in a lot better shape than he was. Since you weigh maybe a hundred and ten or fifteen pounds, I can't see you as that opponent."

She frowned. "Hardly."

"And guns are my hobby," the lieutenant continued. "I'm considered something of an expert. If my educated guess is right, the man was shot with a .357 Magnum, not the kind of gun a woman your size would be likely to carry around in her purse."

Peggy shook her head. "Not me, anyway. I've never even held a gun." Relief flooded through her, but now that he seemed in a talkative mood she didn't want to let him stop. "Randall told me he'd left a message on Mr. Tyler's answering machine at home, saying his appointment had been postponed and he'd be leaving the cabin yesterday morning." He nodded, indicating he'd already known this. "According to what Mr. Tyler told me, his wife left San Francisco yesterday morning. He said he'd talked to her and she had a day full of appointments. Why didn't she tell her husband about Randall's message on the answering machine?"

The lieutenant fought back a grin. "Mrs. Tyler says she rarely ever plays back that recorder. It's connected to a separate phone number in Mr. Tyler's home office. Anyway, she claims she had a very busy day and didn't get around to listening to it until late yesterday. By the time her husband called her at five and she gave him Mr. Barker's message, you were already on your way up here and they couldn't reach you."

Peggy digested that piece of information. It sounded all right. That was probably how Mrs. Tyler knew where to locate Randall. The lieutenant interrupted her thinking. "Are you having trouble with that, Miss Hale?"

"No, I guess not. I *am* wondering why Mr. Tyler gave me that story about being in San Francisco when he apparently wasn't."

"That I can't answer. We'll be checking on his activities in San Francisco. His wife left him up there at eight yesterday morning. She says she thought he was in San Francisco when he called her at noon and again at five. We'll attempt to find out how he spent the day." He dropped his eyelids. "If you have no further questions, Miss Hale, I'll get on with my work."

She felt the sting and stood up. Nick spoke up. "Bob, I have one."

The lieutenant frowned. "Not you too, Nick?"

Nick shrugged. "I guess it's catching. Did Mrs. Tyler say why they were in San Francisco?"

"She claims she was there to do some shopping and her husband had some business to take care of. She says she doesn't know much about his business."

Peggy clucked her tongue. "I'd question that, lieutenant. She worked for Mr. Tyler before they were married about nine or ten years ago. That's the word at the office, anyway. It's said she quit about a year after they married. Randall can probably tell you more. He bought into the company seven or eight years ago when Mr. Tyler wanted to expand and needed money." The lieutenant raised an eyebrow but didn't comment. She went on, "Did you find the note I left in the door last night?"

He stood up and nodded. "Yes, Miss Hale, we found your note. It was on the floor just inside the door."

"That proves someone was there after we left, doesn't it?"

"Not necessarily, but for now we'll accept it." The lieutenant ushered them out of his office to a long counter. "They should have your statements ready for you to sign shortly. Now remember, you two, you're not to leave the county without advising me."

They both nodded, and then Peggy thought of one more thing. "Lieutenant, does anyone know if Mr. Tyler could call from an outside phone and get his messages from his answering machine? I think you can do that on almost all of those machines these days."

He almost laughed. "His wife says he never does, but we'll check further, Miss Hale, I assure you. Now I'll say good-bye." He turned, walked back into his office, and closed the door.

She looked at Nick. "I don't think he fell in love with me."

Nick laughed. "Maybe not, but I don't think he minds your questions as much as he'd like you to think. Bob Watson is a nice guy and a good cop. I've known him for a long time. I don't think he feels you had anything to do with the murder, no matter what Mrs. Tyler claims."

"Whew!"

Nick laughed again. "Yeah, whew! You never did seem worried, though."

She looked at him and grimaced. "The word *murder* and the name Peggy Sue Hale in the same sentence has to be a mistake. I even mourn dead flowers."

After they had read and signed their statements, Nick cupped her elbow in his hand and steered her toward his car. "There's a little café down the road that serves great deli sandwiches. I'm hungry."

"I'm starved," she said, holding her stomach. Answering so many questions and having Jennifer Tyler watching her like a hawk all morning had kept Peggy's stomach tied in a knot. Now, with her statement signed and Jennifer Tyler on her way back to San Diego, Peggy began to relax. She remembered she had eaten only a chicken sandwich the night before and had forgone breakfast to get up to the cabin before seven o'clock.

She sat down at a table covered with a blue-and-white checked tablecloth and let out a long breath before saying, "With all that's gone on this morning, I haven't taken even a minute to mourn Mr. Tyler's death. When it does sink in, I know I'll be devastated. After all, I worked with the man every day. But I'm glad my involvement is over no matter what Mrs. Tyler thinks."

"We'll hope so, but don't be too sure. We don't know what the lieutenant is *really* thinking."

Chapter Three

During lunch, Peggy and Nick discussed everything that had happened that morning. As they were about to leave the café, Peggy frowned. "I'm wondering about that red sports car. The lieutenant said it was rented."

Nick opened the door for her and followed her outside. "Yeah, the license-plate frames are from a car-rental agency in La Jolla that specializes in renting expensive cars. I heard Bobby Linden, one of the deputies, say that there were no papers in the glove compartment and that the car was showroom clean. No fingerprints."

Peggy shoved her hands into the pockets of her jeans. "The only time I ever rented a car, I kept all the endless papers they gave me in the glove compartment in case I had an accident or something."

"Most of us do. Whoever rented that car didn't. It's odd that it's the same make, model, and year as Randall's."

"I guess someone wanted everyone to think Randall was still here after he left."

Nick started his car but didn't move. "Why would someone want to do that?"

She made a face. "I was wondering that too."

He eased his car out of the parking space. "It seems to me that you were just a pawn in all of this. I have an idea something rather dramatic was supposed to happen with that attaché case—something that backfired."

"Did it ever," she said, dramatically drawing her hand across her forehead.

Nick drove back to the Tyler cabin, where Peggy had left her car. When they arrived, Mr. Kolby, the man who lived across the road, was out in his yard. Peggy leaped out of Nick's car as soon as it stopped and ran over to Mr. Kolby. She told him who she was and what had gone on that morning. "Mr. Kolby, would you mind telling me what time you heard those shots last night?"

The stooped, white-haired man was delighted with the information she gave him. "I wondered what was going on over there this morning. But once I knew Tyler had been murdered and all the other cars started to arrive, I decided to go into the house. I didn't want to seem like a nosy old neighbor."

Peggy made a face. "I don't know how you resisted. I wouldn't have been able to. Mr. Kolby, what time did you hear the shots?"

"Well, we were watching television when we heard the first shots. We think there were three, but they were a couple of minutes apart during a game show that has lots of bells ringing. I guess it was between seven-thirty and eight."

"You said the first shots. When did you hear more shots?"

"Let me see, we were watching a cop show that came on at ten. Guns are always going off in one of those shows, you know. But during a commercial I heard what I think were a couple of other shots, one right after another. They weren't very clear. As I told the sheriff's deputy, at the time I didn't think they were gunshots, but later I knew they had to be."

She nodded. "I arrived around seven-thirty, so those earlier shots were probably the ones fired at me. I didn't hear a third shot, but the man may have followed me into the trees. When I ran through those woods, I was too panicked to hear much of anything except my racing heart."

"I don't doubt that, young lady."

"Did you see any cars clearly?"

"No, not so I'd recognize them. I just heard all the traffic out here when there's usually none at all. That man with the red sports car was up here for a couple of days and I'd seen him walking around, but I didn't see him yesterday. I didn't notice his car there yesterday until about five o'clock, when I heard a car go by while we were eating. Then a bit later, I heard a car start up. That's when I looked out and saw a sporty car go by. The red car was still by the house. Right after that a small tan car drove in."

"That was me." She pointed to her car.

Mr. Kolby nodded. "Well, just about the time it started to rain, I thought I heard someone running down the road, but I couldn't be sure. We have a few people up here who run for exercise. I didn't give it much thought, except that all the activity was a lot for this street at this time of year."

Peggy took in a deep breath. "Thank you, Mr. Kolby, for answering my questions."

"Not at all. You know, the real traffic started later, after the rain began to ease off and after I saw the sheriff's car and you and Nick leave."

"Oh?" He had her undivided attention.

"Well, right after you all left, another car went down the road, stopped at Tyler's, and left after only a few minutes. Maybe an hour or more later I heard another car go by. It was there quite a while, I think. The eleven o'clock news was almost over when I heard it leave. I didn't see it, but my wife thought it was that sports car again. Then about midnight another car came in. I didn't see it, either, but I know it didn't stay long. It's usually so quiet up here at night, you can hear a cat walk on gravel." He chuckled. "You know, I never saw a light over there the whole time. Since there's no place to go beyond Tyler's place, I thought something fishy was going on. It was after midnight when I called the sheriff. That last car took off like a shot when it left."

Nick had followed her to Mr. Kolby's yard

and had taken in the whole conversation. When they left the man, Nick chuckled. "Who says life in the country is dull?"

"Yeah, who indeed? I wonder if the person who shot Mr. Tyler was the same one who beat him up."

"Maybe the coroner will be able to answer that question. Do you feel you learned much?"

"Yeah, that this little dirt road was like a free-way last night."

He chuckled. "I guess. It sounds like that red car arrived before five. Then there was a sports car that came and went. After we left there was another car that didn't stay long, and an hour or so later, another car arrived—maybe the sports car again—and stayed awhile. About midnight another one arrived but didn't stay long and left in a big hurry." He shrugged and looked over at her. "Do you have to go back to San Diego now? You could come over to my place and we could put on some tapes or take a walk."

It was tempting. "I thought you wanted to listen to your beard grow."

He smiled quite nicely. "I can do that tomorrow."

She looked at her watch. "It's three-thirty. I'd better head home. Thanks for the invitation, but it looks like it might start raining again."

"Okay, but you don't know what you're missing. I'll call you next week and see if they've set a date for your arraignment."

"If they do, I'll probably be on the eleven o'clock news."

He laughed. "Okay, if I don't see you on the eleven o'clock news, I'll call you at your office. Maybe we can have dinner."

She was smiling as she drove down the dirt road to Sunrise Highway. Nick Donovan was very nice indeed. She opened the window and took a deep breath of the clean, wood-scented air. She did it several times until she turned onto Highway 8 and headed west, back to San Diego. Although she felt saddened by Mr. Tyler's death, she couldn't deny being relieved that her involvement was over. She idly wondered if Nick would call her.

Peggy woke early the next morning. It wasn't easy to concentrate on the mundane routine she usually followed on a gloomy Sunday. Somehow, her apartment got cleaned, her nails got polished, and the laundry got washed and ironed.

The newspaper carried the story of Mr. Tyler's death. The story about Peggy's call from Mr. Tyler lent a further air of mystery to the death of a man who was supposed to be in San Francisco.

Peggy was thankful that her parents were out of town for a few days. Her mother had been devastated when Peggy's twenty-two-year-old sister eloped on Thursday with the man she'd been going with since high school. Peggy's mother had been planning their wedding for years. Peggy's father had shrewdly whisked his wife away to Mazatlán early on Friday morning to recover, saying they'd be back when they returned. With any luck, they would not hear about Mr. Tyler's murder in Mazatlán. By the time they returned home, she hoped, everything would be cleared up.

Peggy thought it was just as well her sister, Amy, would also be away on her Hawaiian honeymoon for two weeks. Like her mother, Amy was prone to instant hysteria that required time, tact, and experience to quiet down.

A few friends called, but Peggy kept the conversations short. It was a little surprising that no one from the office called. But although she was friendly with almost everyone in the firm, Peggy had formed no close friendships with her fellow workers.

The phone rang just after noon. "Peggy Hale?" the man asked in a smooth radio announcer's voice.

"Yes," she answered hesitantly.

"My name is Scott Tyler. I'm Fred Tyler's nephew." He hesitated just a moment. "I've just arrived from LA. My Aunt Jennifer is quite upset, and my father says that she accused you of killing my uncle. My father and I feel you deserve an apology, and I'd like to deliver it. I'd also like to talk to you, if I may. If you haven't eaten, maybe we can have lunch. I'll admit I don't know San Diego very well, but I'm wondering if we could meet somewhere."

Peggy clenched her teeth for a moment. How did she know who this man really was? She hadn't even known that Mr. Tyler had a brother, let alone a nephew. She cleared her throat. If she met him in some very public place she might be able to learn something herself. "Where are you?"

"I'm at my uncle's house out on Point Loma."

She thought for a moment and then remembered a coffee shop on Point Loma Boulevard. She gave him directions. "It will take me about a half hour. How will I know you?"

He laughed lightly. "I'll be the tall, thin, good-looking, black-haired man standing outside the restaurant waiting for you."

She closed her eyes for a moment. "I'll recognize you by your humility. I'll be wearing jeans and a red-and-white sweater." She hung up the phone and groaned. Undoubtedly, he'd be a laugh a minute. She checked her lipstick, grabbed her shoulder bag, and left.

Scott Tyler was indeed the tall, thin, good-looking, black-haired man who stood by the door of the coffee shop. He greeted her in an open, friendly manner that might have caught her off guard under different circumstances. After he apologized for Jennifer Tyler's behavior and they ordered lunch, he frowned deeply. "You know, everything I've heard doesn't make much sense."

Peggy nodded. "There's little that makes sense to me."

"You know nothing about the newspapers in the attaché case?"

"Not a thing." His interest centered mostly on the attaché case and the man who had shot at her. She answered his questions without elaborating on anything. She was trying to make up her mind about him. He appeared to be intelligent, well educated, and well mannered. He also appeared to be genuinely concerned. When there was a lull in their conversation, she asked him something that was bothering her. "Scott, did you know your uncle well?"

He leaned back in the booth and smiled. "No, I didn't know him at all, really. I'll admit to a slight curiosity about the guy, though. He and my father had a falling-out years ago, according to my paternal grandmother, and they never came out of it. According to my dad, their falling-out came after their father died, but I've never been certain just what it was about. Dad's always been vague on the subject. My grandmother would never give me direct answers, either. Fred and my father were only half-brothers, you know."

Peggy shook her head. "No, I didn't know, but I didn't even know Mr. Tyler had a brother."

After they decided they couldn't enlighten

each other about what had really happened up at the cabin, Scott leaned back and cocked his head. "What do you do at Tyler Advertising?"

"I'm general manager, and I work on layouts for our advertising campaigns. I'm not an artist or a photographer, but I work with their work. What do you do?"

"I work for my father in his investment firm. I'm thirty, but in that line of work I'm still considered wet behind the ears. I'll like it better if they ever decide I can think for myself. You always have to do twice as well as anyone else to be considered adequate when you work for your father." He grinned sheepishly.

Peggy hesitated to admit she liked Scott. There was something of the little boy grown tall in him. They talked of their careers and families, which surprised her, since she wasn't one given to personal conversations with people she didn't know well. Just before they parted in the parking lot, Scott looked down at her and gave her a dazzling smile. "Peggy, I don't know how long I'll be in San Diego, but I'd like to see you again before I leave, if we can work it out."

She smiled more broadly than she meant to. "We can play it by ear."

On the way back to her apartment, Peggy thought about her meeting with Scott. Why he had wanted to talk to her wasn't too clear. He was interested only in the attaché case and the man who shot at her. He did apologize for Mrs.

Tyler's behavior, but. . . . Maybe there was something she hadn't picked up on. She'd try to analyze him more later.

She turned onto the street she lived on and noticed a small black car turn in behind her. She had sensed that it had been following her on her way to the restaurant but had decided it had been her imagination. When she pulled into the parking lot of her apartment building, the small black car slowed down but went on. When she got out of her car, she looked around but didn't see the car again. Chalking up her uneasiness to paranoia, she went inside.

Peggy watched the news on TV while she ate a frozen dinner guaranteed to be low in calories. She hoped there had been some new developments uncovered about Mr. Tyler's murder. The newsman said little was known about the murderer or his motive. At least she wasn't mentioned as a suspect. She flinched at the thought of a reporter talking to Mrs. Tyler. The woman would probably be quite free with her feelings about her, Peggy thought. *Mother, please stay in Mazatlán,* she prayed.

Peggy eyed the phone and wondered if Nick was still up in the mountains or if he'd returned home. Maybe he'd learned something since she left there. She'd already looked up his number in the phone book. He lived only a couple of blocks away in a new apartment complex. As she played with the idea of calling him, the phone rang.

She grabbed the phone quickly. Before she could say anything, a man spoke in a gravelly voice that closely resembled Mr. Tyler's. "Miss Hale, we know you switched the attaché case. That's our money you have and we expect to get it. We know you've probably stashed it somewhere. You wouldn't be dumb enough to keep it in your apartment. We'll join you, when the time is right, and you can take us to our two hundred fifty thousand dollars. If you're interested in seeing your twenty-fifth birthday, you won't tell anyone of this call." The phone went dead.

Without breathing, she stared at the phone. Two hundred fifty thousand dollars! Someone was out of his mind. And that voice . . . it sounded so much like Mr. Tyler's. No one had even hinted that the body in that cabin wasn't his. *Was someone trying to frighten me by imitating his voice?* she thought. At the risk of jeopardizing her twenty-fifth birthday, she considered calling the lieutenant.

She hung up the phone, walked over to the window, and stared out at the darkness. Surely whoever had called would realize he was wrong. If there was that kind of money involved in all this, Peggy couldn't imagine who might have it. If it was supposed to be in that attaché case she took from the safe. . . . Preposterous! She frowned and turned from the window. Why were those newspapers in that attaché case? Lillian said Mr. Tyler had placed that case in the safe the night before he left for San Francisco. Where were the Calloway files? She made a mental note to check on them first thing in the morning.

Television didn't help her state of mind. The fact that she was involved in all this made her livid. She reached for the phone and dialed. Nick answered on the second ring. She blurted out her story about the phone call. He was silent for a minute, then asked softly, "Peggy, where do you live?" She gave him her address. "We're almost neighbors. I'll be right over."

Maybe talking to someone about this turn of events would help. Peggy didn't usually feel the need to discuss her personal problems with anyone. In fact, she never liked to admit she had a problem—an attitude that always bugged her mother and her sister. But after that threatening phone call, she acknowledged that this was one problem she couldn't handle alone.

Her mind started going over things. Why would that kind of money be in that attaché case? What was supposed to happen to it? Was Randall Barker being truthful in saying he knew nothing about the attaché case? If so, what had Mr. Tyler been up to? She went into the kitchen, put on a pot of coffee, and took cookies out of the freezer.

It briefly occurred to her that it might be foolish to tell Nick everything. After all, she didn't know him. He was only indirectly involved in all this, wasn't he? It flashed into her mind that he had briefly been alone with that attaché case while she'd dried off in his bathroom. He had a sports car, and Mr. Kolby had said there was a sports car at the cabin. She closed her eyes and questioned her sanity. Nick had nothing to do with all this. But he had been in the woods when she ran through them!

A knock on the door interrupted her thoughts.

Nick started talking as soon as he entered her apartment. "I called the sheriff's station up at Mt. Laguna, but Bob Watson is off tonight. He's not at home, either. They're probably out to dinner. He has a couple of small kids, so it's not likely they'll be out late." He turned around and picked up her hand. "You okay?"

She looked up into his concerned eyes, which she noticed were very blue. All her vague doubts about him vanished into thin air. By coming so quickly, he was proving he was one of the good guys, wasn't he? "I guess so," she said, "but I'm furious, if you want to know the truth. I hate it that I'm involved in this, whatever it is. And that voice sounded just like Mr. Tyler's. It sent chills up and down my spine. And the idea of all that money. . . ."

He squeezed her hand. "Yeah, it's weird, all right. I do know there was no doubt that it was Tyler's body up there in that cabin, if that's what you're wondering about." He dropped her hand and sat down on the couch. "By the way, I checked and found out that planes were grounded in San Francisco on Friday after three-thirty. Tyler must have been somewhere locally when he called you. In fact, everything suggests that our Mr. Tyler, victim though he was, was not necessarily a pillar of the community." He appeared to be thinking as he talked.

Peggy watched him for a minute before she spoke. "I know one thing. Mrs. Tyler wasn't answering her phone Friday night. I called there twice after I got home. I left my name on the answering machine, and she never called me back." She bit her lip.

Nick raised his eyebrows. "Interesting. She said she was home alone, watching TV all evening. By the way, Bob told me that Randall Barker and his estranged wife were having a long leisurely dinner out on Shelter Island that night. They're working on a reconciliation, they say. They happen to be well known at that restaurant." He shrugged.

"You've been busy," she said, relaxing a little. "The Barkers have been separated for some time." She changed the subject. "I've found out that if things had gone as planned, I'd have delivered two hundred fifty thousand dollars to someone—but who? And why? And . . . where is the money?"

"Yeah, the more questions I think of, the more that come to mind." Nick looked up at her and grinned. "By the way, Tyler died between ten and midnight, and his death was caused by a mean gash on the back of his head, not the gunshots.

That information isn't being released. I overheard it at the sheriff's station this morning, and Bob Watson swore me to secrecy. I'm betting I can trust you, obviously." He grinned again. "I saw some of the photos. There was a big gash on the back of his head and a lot of blood by his head but hardly any blood around the bullet holes. At least some time elapsed between the beating and the gunshots. He bled a lot internally."

Peggy shivered. "I don't need to know the gory details. He could have been lying there bleeding while I was banging on the door." She shivered again. "I wonder if he could have been trying to call to me while I banged on the door and called to Randall. Or maybe when we went back. . . ." She sucked in her breath. "Maybe if I'd listened more closely. . . ."

Nick glared at her. "Now, don't go giving yourself a load of guilt. You had absolutely no way of knowing if he was even there when you were at the door. When we returned with the deputies, you and I were at the door only to put your note there. No one heard anything that time, and the deputies aimed their flashlights in the windows and didn't see anything." He sounded annoyed.

Peggy closed her eyes and turned toward the kitchen. "Before you tell me more, I think I'll get us some coffee."

Nick looked up at her. "Oh, I do have more to tell you."

Chapter Four

Peggy returned to the living room with mugs of coffee and a plate of cookies. Nick absently picked up a cookie and bit into it. He pulled his head back and looked at the cookie. "It's frozen."

"I keep them in the freezer. It's the only place they're safe from me. Tell me, did you learn anything else before you left the mountain?"

Nick continued looking at the cookie, broke off a small bite, and went on. "Yes. I'd intended to call you, but you beat me to it." He looked up at her and smiled. "I'm glad you did. It makes me feel you want me here." His smile disappeared. "Bob Watson was right about the kind of gun that was used. It was a big .357 Magnum. That's not a lady's gun. He thinks there's a possibility that Tyler had two visitors that night. When Harry Pike, the deputy, arrived after Mr. Kolby's call, the front door was unlocked, a fact that suggests Tyler may have let someone in. The back-door lock had been shot off, and of course that suggests someone forced his way in."

"It sure does. I'm glad those deputies checked everything. That puts us in the clear."

"Not necessarily." He raised his eyebrows suddenly. "What do you mean, *us?* You're the one the widow wants to hang." He broke into a broad grin and then turned serious again. "You know Mr. Kolby said another car drove in shortly after we left. If someone wanted to make something out of it, he could say you returned. Mrs. Tyler wants to involve you in the worst way. Have you two had difficulty?"

Peggy waved her hand in the air. "Not at all. I've only met the woman a couple of times." She sat forward in her chair. "I'd like to take a walk around the grounds."

"You'd what?"

"I'm edgy. I think some air might help."

Nick stood up. "Whatever you say."

There was a chill in the air, but it felt good. Peggy took several deep breaths and let them out slowly. She wondered if she should tell Nick about her meeting with Scott Tyler. After all, she had told him almost everything else. She decided to risk telling him.

He didn't comment for a minute. When he did, he asked softly, "What does he look like?"

She described him briefly. "He looks a little like his father."

"Could he have been the one who shot at you?"

Peggy laughed. "I doubt it. In the first place, he's quite thin. Why do you ask?"

"You said that the man was taller than Randall Barker and that Scott Tyler was quite interested in the man who shot at you."

She didn't want to admit it was something to think about. The man *had* worn a coat. She really had no idea of his build, now that she thought about it. "I think he was just curious. Also, I think one of his main purposes in meeting with me was to apologize for Jennifer's behavior. He mentioned two or three times that his father had been angry at her for accusing me the way she did." Peggy wasn't yet sure how she felt about Scott Tyler. Nick didn't comment, so she changed the subject. "Someone could have shot the lock off the back door, beat up Mr. Tyler, shot him, and left by the front door, leaving it unlocked."

Nick nodded. "Yeah, but there's also a possibility that the person who beat him up and the one who shot him were not one and the same. Remember that Mr. Kolby said someone was there before you arrived. One car came right after we left with the deputies but didn't stay long. Then another car came an hour or so later and stayed awhile. And one came about midnight."

Peggy shook her head. "He had a lot of company if he was already dead."

Nick nodded. "The other scenario I've dreamt up says that he let the person he fought with in the front door. After the guy knocked him out, he left. Then someone else came, shot off the lock on the back door, went in, found Tyler on the floor, didn't know he was dead, and shot him."

Peggy swallowed. "Would you know if someone was dead?"

"Yes, I think so."

"I'm not sure I would. On TV I've seen them check for a pulse in the neck, but I'm not sure I'd find it if it was there. I can't find my own half the time." She placed her fingers on her neck. "I must have passed on. I can't find a pulse."

They stopped and Nick placed two fingers on her neck. They felt nice and warm. "Good news. You're still here."

"Whew," she said and started to walk on.

"Tell me what you know about Tyler," Nick said, glancing around the dark parking lot.

"When you put it that way, not much. The only time I've ever seen him outside the office was at the cabin when he held a barbecue this past summer. All the employees and a few old clients were there." She shrugged.

"What about the office grapevine?"

She made a face. "It's busy. Mrs. Tyler gets seen every so often at some restaurant with someone who doesn't even resemble Mr. Tyler. If she does have boyfriends, she'll never take honors for discretion. There is one thing, though."

"Oh?" Nick picked up her hand.

His warm hand felt good. Again, she questioned the intelligence of telling Nick so much, but went on anyway. "Well, Mr. Tyler handled a few old accounts, but Randall oversees most of the work we do and he takes care of all the field-work. Everyone thinks Randall works a lot harder than Mr. Tyler ever did. Anyway, about once a month or so, without any regularity, Mr. Tyler would leave the office in the middle of the morning. He always said, 'I'll be back when I get back.' He never said where he was going."

"How long had it been going on?"

Peggy bit her lip. "About a year, I'd say. I may be able to get something out of Lillian, his secretary. He usually came back about the middle of the next morning. Of course, being a partner in the business, he could do as he pleased, but it always caused a lot of talk. Normally he never left the office. He even had his lunch sent in. He spent a lot of time on the phone." She shrugged. "Some people thought he might be seeing a woman, but he just never seemed the type to me."

"Some say there is no type, only opportunity."

"So I've heard."

They walked into the lighted courtyard. They had seen no one since they stepped outside. "When did he leave for San Francisco?" Nick asked.

"He and his wife left Tuesday morning and were supposed to return Friday afternoon."

Nick frowned. "Did Tyler ever say anything to you about his personal life?"

She shook her head. "No, we never talked about anything except business. He paid me well, gave me good bonuses at Christmas, and was usually quite considerate, but we never said anything personal to each other."

When they walked around the front of the building, they stopped. A man was hurrying away from Nick's car. They called to him, but he disappeared into the darkness and the shrubbery. Nick ran after him, but stopped at the row of oleanders that lined the driveway. Beyond was a busy street, and there was no sign of the man. They went back to Nick's car but found no evidence of tampering. Peggy shivered. "Let's go in. I need a cup of coffee."

He slipped his arm around her waist. "Me too."

The phone rang just as they opened the door of her apartment. They looked at each other for a moment without moving. Peggy spoke first. "It could be my parents. They've been away for a few days. Maybe they've heard about Mr. Tyler."

Nick nodded. "Let me listen until you're sure."

She picked up the phone with more than a little apprehension. It was the gravelly voice again. "I can see you're not overly concerned with your twenty-fifth birthday, Miss Hale. We know your boyfriend is there, and we're sure you're telling him all. Unless you want to jeopardize his next birthday too, you'd better follow our orders and make sure he doesn't say anything to anyone."

Peggy clenched her teeth. Her temper flared.

She knew she should be intimidated, but she just couldn't feel it. "You're watching me! How dare you? Now you listen to me. If you're so sure I have all that money, I know you won't jeopardize my twenty-fifth birthday or anyone else's birthday in case I decide to give it all to the police. If you're so smart, you know this isn't the sort of thing I do for a living."

"Cute, Miss Hale, very cute. You might remember this. If you turn it in to the police, you'll be admitting you stole it. Mrs. Tyler will press charges. Bet on it. She's sure you're in on her husband's murder, but she has no proof." The man chuckled. "Another thing. If you try to bluff your way with the police by telling them about these calls and saying you don't have the money, you'll plant a seed. They'll begin to wonder about you too. They'll wonder why someone thinks you switched the attaché cases. They'll probably start watching your every move." The man chuckled and the phone went dead.

Nick pried the phone from her clenched hand and hung it up. He pulled her into his arms. "You're gutsy when you get riled, aren't you?"

She was shaking with anger and a fear she wanted to deny. His strong body felt warm and steady, and his arms around her helped a lot. "Somehow, they're watching me. How?"

"They're probably watching the building and saw us take our little stroll around the grounds." He squeezed her shoulders.

"What I said may not have been brilliant, but if they killed me, they'd lose the chance of finding the money, if they really believe I have it. And threatening to hurt you. . . ." She looked up at him, knowing she was out of her league. "Well, couldn't we just split, or something? No one who's ever known me could ever conceive of me doing anything illegal." Tears rushed into her eyes.

Nick pulled her to him again and held her firmly for a moment. He rubbed her back and murmured into her hair, "Go ahead and cry. You're right. You're not the criminal type."

Her sobbing subsided, and she pulled her head back and looked up at him. He smiled down at her. His eyes twinkled. In unison, they burst into laughter. When she stopped laughing, she brushed away the tears and reluctantly turned away from him. "Nick, what am I going to do? They *really* believe I have the money. I'm so angry."

Nick walked over to her and kissed her forehead. "I think you're frightened too, but you don't want to admit it. Trust me. I won't let anything happen to you."

"I am not frightened. I'm mad. I'm furious that this situation has invaded my life." She hadn't meant to raise her voice.

His smile annoyed her further, but he spoke softly. "You have a right to be frightened, you know. In fact, you should admit it to yourself even if you don't want to admit it to me." He reached for the phone. "I'm going to see if Bob Watson is home yet. A lieutenant in the sheriff's department should know more about the criminal types than we do. If he doesn't, I have a few ideas of my own."

Lieutenant Bob Watson listened as Nick reported Peggy's phone calls. She wasn't thoroughly convinced telling the police was the right thing to do, but she didn't have a good argument against it. She didn't believe for a minute that the lieutenant would think she stole that money, no matter what the phone callers said. She listened in and said nothing. It was a moment before the lieutenant responded. "I can ask the San Diego department to give her police protection."

Peggy gasped. "Really, lieutenant, I don't think that's necessary. I can't see that I'd be in jeopardy before they got their money, no matter what they say. I think they're just trying to scare me, and they're doing an admirable job."

Again he hesitated before he spoke. "Do you live alone, Miss Hale?"

"Yes, I do."

"Could you stay with someone?"

"I suppose so, but I'd hate to bring anyone else into this."

"I can understand that. Look, I don't want you to leave your apartment by yourself. I'll advise the San Diego police and have them contact you."

"Lieutenant, I have to go into the office tomorrow."

Nick spoke up. "I'll drive her there, Bob." He looked at her and winked. She frowned. This was getting out of hand.

"Good," the lieutenant said. "Peggy, you be sure to keep your doors locked. Do you have a dead bolt?"

He sounded like her father. "Yes. I—"

The lieutenant cut her off. "For the time being, don't mention these calls to *anyone*. If you still want to go through the cabin, I'll take you through tomorrow. You may pick up on something being odd that we didn't see."

"I'd like that. Will four tomorrow afternoon be okay?"

"Four will be fine," the lieutenant answered.

Nick jumped in before she could say more. "We'll be there at four." He hung up the phone and grinned at her. "He may not have fallen in love with you, but he likes you. He called you Peggy. He rarely calls people by their first names unless he knows them well and really likes them."

Peggy sighed dramatically. "I'll settle for *like* from the lieutenant. I feel guilty, but I'm so angry at Mr. Tyler for getting me into this mess."

Nick pulled her down on the couch beside him, picked up her hands, and squeezed them. "I think we can safely say that things didn't go according to Mr. Tyler's plan, whatever it might have been. Don't worry, I'll make sure nothing happens to you. I plan to stick to you like glue. Here's what I think you should do." He leaned over and kissed her lightly on the forehead.

A tinge of excitement mixed with her fear and anger, but the anger prevailed. She leaped to her feet. "Okay, we'd better get something straight. I don't need a sitter or a protector or whatever. I can take care of myself, thank you. I'm not going to run around scared of anything or anyone. I never have and I don't plan to start now. I haven't done anything, for heaven's sake. I don't need a chauffeur to get to work in the morning, either. In my car, between seven-thirty and eight o'clock in the morning, on the streets of San Diego, I feel quite safe, thank you. Now, you'd better leave. I should get to bed." She hadn't meant to be so abrupt.

He pulled her to him, kissed her ardently, and then gave her a mischievous grin. He walked toward the door. "I knew there'd be sparks when I did that. Be sure and throw the dead bolt when I leave. I'll see you in the morning."

Peggy stared at the closed door after he left. Sparks, indeed. She threw the dead bolt and turned away before she acknowledged to herself that her heart was racing.

* * *

A fat lot of good my outburst did, she thought the next morning when Nick showed up at her door a little after seven. She started to protest, but the clock told her she didn't have time for a discussion. It would be easier to let him drive her to the office. In the cold, hard light of morning, the whole situation seemed ludicrous, but a man was dead and someone was looking for a lot of money supposedly in her possession.

Nick kept glancing in his rearview mirror. "I think we're being followed by a big black car." He stopped at the curb in front of her office building and let her out. She hurried into the lobby and turned to watch Nick pull away from the curb. A big black car followed him. A chill ran down her spine.

When she entered the offices of Tyler Advertising, the place was buzzing and all eyes were on her. Lillian Frye called to her before she reached her own office. As soon as Peggy stepped into Lillian's office, the older woman started talking. "I told you that you shouldn't be so quick to say you'd go up to the cabin. We all heard about Mr. Tyler. Wait until you see what's waiting for you." She gestured toward Mr. Tyler's office. "They said they wanted to see you as soon as you arrived."

Peggy walked into the big office tentatively. Jennifer Tyler and Randall Barker were standing by the big desk. Off to one side was Mr. Tyler's brother, a slim man with blond hair, cold green eyes, and a neck brace. Now that she thought about it, he seemed to have taken pains to keep his distance from her both at the cabin and at the sheriff's station on Saturday. Scott stood off to the other side. He nodded to her and almost smiled. No one else wore the suggestion of a smile.

Jennifer Tyler's eyes flashed. She was her usual impeccably made-up self, her red hair perfectly in place. She was dressed in a black, body-skimming jumpsuit. "Peggy, I want you to know that even though that hick sheriff up in the mountains won't arrest you, I still think you're involved in my husband's murder. I intend to prove it," she said.

Peggy dropped her bag to the floor. "Mrs. Tyler. . . ." She wanted to yell at her, but she worked to control her voice. "I did not have anything to do with your husband's death."

Randall laid his hand on Jennifer's arm. He looked at Peggy and shook his head slightly. "Jennifer's upset, Peggy."

"I'm sure she is, but—"

Jennifer Tyler cut in. "I don't think you should be allowed to continue working here, but Randall says he needs you."

"I most certainly do," Randall said, sounding bored. "We're gathering up Fred's things, Peggy." They were pulling folders from the file cabinet beside his desk. "Lillian says his personal files are all here."

For a moment, Peggy felt as though Mr. Tyler's personal life was being violated by people who shouldn't have access to it. She resented their intrusion. Also, they were foiling her own plans. She had an idea that there might be something in those personal files that would point to a questionable involvement of some kind. She had figured a way to get by Lillian and take a look. So much for that idea. But there had to be something somewhere that would give a clue to whatever was behind a beating, a shooting, and the disappearance of a large sum of money.

Randall looked at the man wearing a neck brace. "Stan, I don't think you've met Peggy. She's our general manager and the best layout person we've had for about three years now." He looked over at her. "Peggy, this is Stan Tyler, Fred's brother. I don't think you two were introduced Saturday."

She nodded to the man, who was older but much more attractive than Mr. Tyler had been. "How do you do, Mr. Tyler," she said.

He almost smiled. "Hello, Peggy," he said softly. He looked over at Scott. "You've met my son, I understand."

"Yes, we've met." She nodded to Scott, who smiled at her before leaning over to help Randall take an armful of folders from the file. They placed them in a large cardboard box.

Randall straightened up and looked at Peggy. "There are a lot of things you and I will have to go over, Peggy. I know you and Fred have been working on that new resort's promos, and the deadline is close. I guess you were also working on the Combo auction TV ads and the new campaign for Sea World. I'm sure there are other things I'll need to be updated on too. I'm going to help Jennifer and Stan today. You take care of things here, and we'll try to get organized tomorrow or the next day. Calm down our edgy clients. I'll make sure you get the calls from Fred's clients. Lillian has many talents, but tact doesn't head the list."

Peggy nodded, picked up her bag, and walked back to her own small office. She set her bag down and reached for the ringing phone. There was little doubt the phone would ring all day. She quickly rehearsed a speech.

An hour later, she was already tired of talking on the phone. Randall called her into Mr. Tyler's office. "We're leaving now, Peg. If it's a real emergency, I'll be at the Tylers' house, but don't tell *anyone.*"

He picked up the large box, and Scott picked up a smaller box. Peggy stepped out of their way just as a tall, muscular man walked into the office and looked at her. "Are you Peggy Hale?" he asked. Lillian was right behind him.

Peggy nodded at the stranger. "Yes, I am."

He flashed a badge and an ID card identifying him as Sergeant Ronald Burke of the San Diego

Police Department; the picture of him was quite good.

She introduced him to Randall. The sergeant spoke in a deep, controlled voice. "May I ask what you have there?" He nodded toward the boxes.

Randall shifted his heavy box and cleared his throat. "These are Mr. Tyler's personal files. His wife wants to take them home." He shifted the box again. "I'd like to put this down if we're going to chat, Sergeant Burke."

"I'd suggest you do that, Mr. Barker. I'm afraid we can't allow anything to be taken from this office for the time being."

Jennifer stepped out from behind Randall. "I demand to be allowed to take my husband's papers home. You have no right to stop me. I'll call my lawyer if you try."

Peggy made a quick introduction. Sergeant Burke nodded. "I'm afraid I do have the right to stop you, Mrs. Tyler. Your husband was murdered, and we check everything in a murder investigation. Also, we've received word that there's a great deal of money involved. Feel free to call your attorney, if you'd like."

She sucked in her breath and narrowed her eyes. She looked at Peggy and then back at the sergeant. "I don't know anything about any money, but this woman probably does. She's the one who was in on the murder of my husband, but that hick sheriff up in the mountains won't do anything. I know she was up at that cabin when my husband was killed."

Sergeant Burke just barely smiled. "The evidence suggests it is quite unlikely that Miss Hale was involved."

"She could have taken someone up there with her to beat him so savagely. She's very friendly with a young man up there, I happen to know. He could have helped her." Jennifer pouted like a defiant child.

"I'm afraid that's speculation, Mrs. Tyler. We go on evidence." He watched Randall and Scott place the cartons on Mr. Tyler's desk.

Stan Tyler stepped forward and introduced himself and his son. "Sergeant, we live in LA and came down Saturday morning after Jennifer called me about my brother's death." He touched his neck brace. "I was in a car wreck a few days ago," he explained. "I'd like to know just how long you intend to tie up my brother's affairs."

His explanation about his neck brace seemed a bit unnecessary. Peggy suspected that the sergeant felt the same way. She had heard or read that it was suspicious when someone answered unasked questions in a situation like this. The sergeant looked at Stan for a long moment before he spoke. "I'm afraid I can't say, Mr. Tyler." He glanced at Randall. "Is there anything in Mr. Tyler's office that is essential to the running of the business for the next few days?"

Randall looked at Peggy. She answered for him. "Not as far as I know right now."

The sergeant nodded. "Okay, then nothing is to be taken from this office unless we say so." He looked around at all of them. "Do you all understand?"

Everyone nodded and Peggy answered, "Yes, of course."

Randall took Jennifer's elbow and ushered her out the door as she continued to rant about her rights and the hick sheriff in the mountains. Sergeant Burke interrupted her. "Mrs. Tyler, I'd like you to come down to the station with me."

Jennifer's head snapped back. "Whatever for?"

The sergeant raised his eyebrows. "That hick sheriff you speak about has learned that the car parked by your cabin up at Mt. Laguna was leased by you. We have a few questions we'd like to ask you about that."

Jennifer's mouth dropped open in a most unattractive manner. Her eyes widened, and she gasped. "But, I didn't. I. . . ." She looked up at Randall and then back at the sergeant.

The sergeant nodded. "Come with me, Mrs. Tyler, and you can tell us about it." He looked down at Peggy. "I'm going to want to talk to you later, Miss Hale. For now, I'd appreciate it if you and Mr. Tyler's secretary would cooperate with our men when they go through his office."

"Of course, sergeant." She gulped.

Lillian came up beside Peggy after the sergeant left with Jennifer Tyler, Randall Barker, and Stan and Scott Tyler. She was disgruntled, as usual. "I can't imagine what Mrs. Tyler's renting a car has to do with anything. Why should they care?"

Peggy filled her in on what she knew. Her instincts told her to stay on Lillian's good side, if possible. Lillian's cooperation wasn't easily won, and Peggy had a sinking feeling she might need it at some point in the not-too-distant future. "I guess the fact that she'd claimed she knew nothing about that car piqued their curiosity. Did you hear that the sergeant wants us to cooperate with his men when they go through Mr. Tyler's things here?"

"I don't know anything about those files in there. He always said that they were strictly personal and that no one was to touch them. He gave me his household bills to pay each month after he checked them over. I wrote the checks. That's all I know about. In the safe there's a spare set of his keys." She spun around and went to her desk.

Peggy looked back into the big office. "I don't imagine they'll need much help from us."

Lillian sat down at her desk and heaved a big sigh. "I have six tapes here to transcribe. With Randall's secretary on vacation, everyone thinks I can do everyone's work."

"Yes, I know, Lillian." Lillian was Tyler Advertising's resident martyr. "Do you have any idea where Mr. Tyler went when he used to leave the office for a day or so?" Peggy wasn't sure she'd answer.

Lillian put on one of her famous deep frowns. "No. He never told me anything he didn't tell everyone."

Peggy bit her lip. "I'm going to check on the Calloway file."

Lillian made a throaty sound. "You'd told me it was supposed to be in the attaché case you took from the safe. I read about the batch of newspapers found in that attaché case you had, so I checked on the Calloway file the first thing this morning. It's in the file cabinet where it belongs. Something awfully funny is going on."

"You've got that right, Lillian." Peggy walked to the door and watched the sergeant herd Jennifer and the men out the double-glass front doors into the hallway, where they were met by a uniformed officer. Why would Jennifer Tyler rent that red car just like Randall's? Two men who had been waiting in the hall spoke to the sergeant. The sergeant nodded in Peggy's direction and left. The two men came toward her and showed her their badges. "The sergeant says you'll give us a hand, Miss Hale."

She nodded and reached for the phone Lillian held out to her. Client Larry Davis expressed his condolences about Mr. Tyler's untimely death and tried to be casual when he mentioned his concern about the deadline for his own advertising campaign. While Peggy listened, she considered trying to find a way to go through Mr. Tyler's papers by herself, without its looking suspicious. If she couldn't, she'd have to come up with a plan B.

After assuring Larry Davis his campaign would not be affected, she turned her attention to the two detectives. They asked her to stay in Mr. Tyler's office while they looked around. She thought Lillian would have been a more appropriate choice, but apparently Lillian and Sergeant Burke had already had a little to-do. It was so easy to get into a fight with Lillian. Peggy rubbed her hands together and shifted from one foot to the other as she watched the men look around without touching a thing. She was delighted when they asked her to look through the files with them.

They asked some good questions, most of which she could answer. Mr. Tyler carried on some personal correspondence with people whose names she recognized. Also, as Lillian had mentioned, he took care of all his household expenses at the office. The folders held everything from utility bills to auto-repair bills. The telephone bills weren't overly large but the top few had a lot of calls to Los Angeles. Only two numbers showed up often. On each bill, in what looked like a woman's handwriting, the names Doris and Ginny were written beside these numbers. While the detective nearest Peggy took a phone call, she jotted down the recurring Los Angeles phone numbers. She wasn't sure what they'd tell her.

Two unmarked folders contained letters to and from the Homer T. Castleberry Company. The letter on top said, *Everything must be cleared by the fifteenth. No more postponements acceptable.* It was a photocopy of a handwritten note. In the other folder were photocopies of handwritten notes to another client and to an accountant Peggy knew only slightly. Why would Mr. Tyler send handwritten notes to clients? Both notes were worded just like the note to Mr. Castleberry. That was interesting, if not revealing. The dates had nothing to do with advertising. The two accounts involved had new campaigns already in production. She studied the notes for a moment.

One of the detectives interrupted her concentration. "Anything wrong, Miss Hale?"

She frowned. "I'm not sure. It strikes me as odd that Mr. Tyler wrote letters to these clients on lined paper with a ballpoint pen. He dictated letters to these clients all the time. I know because I've worked on their layouts and he's often had me look at the letters to make sure he didn't leave out anything." Her mind was spinning.

One of the men looked over her shoulder. "Are these letters more personal?"

"Yes, although I'm not sure why. For instance,

I've never seen correspondence with a salutation of 'Dear Ben' on a letter to J. Bently Ashton. Down here at the bottom are J. Bently's initials and his address." She looked at him and grinned. "I hardly call him Ben."

The detective smiled. "Very few do that I know about. J. Bently pushes a lot of buttons in this town, but maybe he and your boss were good friends. Frankly I don't know what his friends call him. The press always refers to him as J. Bently when they're trying to be informal."

Peggy nodded and replaced the letter. "Mr. Tyler referred to him that way too. We've had his bank's advertising account forever, I think." She glanced at the other letters in that folder. She wanted to go through those folders again. What else might be there that didn't go through the office channels? Why keep these separate files for clients? She glanced at the man beside her and shrugged.

The detective nodded. "Could this just be something to do with some advertising deadlines for these men? Maybe he was macho enough to think a handwritten note from him would get them on the ball."

Peggy shrugged. "Who knows?" She didn't believe it for a minute, but she didn't have any concrete reason she could tell the detective.

"We'll be through here in about an hour," he said. "I think the sergeant will be back by then.

He'll probably want to take a look too." He gestured at the boxes of folders on the desk.

When he walked away from the desk, she glanced at the calendar. Friday, the day Mr. Tyler was killed, was the fifteenth. She scribbled down the names of the people those letters were written to. If she couldn't get to that folder again, maybe she'd be able to find out something in their office files.

She went through more files. Each of the next four folders had a long, sealed envelope with something stiff inside and the name of a different bank on the outside. Not knowing whether she was within her rights to do so, and not really considering the matter very much, she opened one envelope. Then she opened the rest. Each envelope contained a bankbook.

She looked up at the detective, who was returning to the desk. "I think this is interesting." She held up one bankbook. Over one hundred thousand dollars had been withdrawn to close the account just a week before. There were six such bankbooks, each from a different bank, each with at least one hundred thousand dollars withdrawn to close the account within the past two weeks. The smallest deposit in any of the bankbooks was twenty thousand dollars. Fred J. Tyler was the only name on each account.

The detective shook his head. "The sergeant will find these pretty interesting, I'm sure."

Peggy didn't doubt it for a minute.

She needed a breather. At the moment she doubted she could be of any further help to the police department. She looked up at the detective, who was studying one of the bankbooks. "Would you mind if I ran to the office next door for a few minutes?" she asked. "I have a personal errand to do there."

He assured her he wouldn't as he picked up another bankbook.

Peggy stepped into the office next door, glad to see that it was empty of clients. Linda Marconi's big eyes lit up. "Oh, Peg, am I glad to see you! I didn't get home until late last night or I'd have called you. I've been dying to talk to you and find out what's going on. Of course I heard about poor Mr. Tyler. And you're involved. Your name was in the paper and—" She sounded ecstatic.

Peggy put up her hand and shook her head. "Hold it. You got a minute?"

"Sure, and besides I'd get fired if I didn't talk to you. My boss's nose is twitching as much as mine. He's asked me three times this morning if I'd seen you yet today. I'd call him out now, but he's on a conference call."

Peggy laughed lightly. "I knew you two would be eager for news." She gave Linda a sketchy report of what happened up at the cabin Friday night and Saturday. "The police are in the office now." She held out a folder. "Linda, please take this paper to class for me tonight. I won't be able to make it."

"You're not being arrested, are you?"

"No, not yet." Peggy fought laughter as Linda's eyes widened again. "Don't get excited. I have to go up and talk to the lieutenant at the sheriff's department at Mt. Laguna this afternoon." She tapped the folder. "I don't want to be late with this. You know Mrs. Goodall isn't thrilled with me, anyway."

"It's only because you stump her so often. You work in the real world of advertising, so you think of things that aren't in the textbooks. It drives her crazy. The rest of us love it."

Peggy made a face. "I should keep my mouth shut, but sometimes I wonder if she knows what goes on in the real world." She took a deep breath. "I hope I make it through her class. Take notes for me tonight, will you?"

"Sure, if I can stay awake. I wish I could work up your enthusiasm for marketing."

Peggy placed her hands on Linda's big impressive desk and leaned forward. "Do you know that little man out there in the hallway reading the newspaper? Our receptionist told me he's been there all morning."

Linda frowned. "No, I don't know who he is, but he should have that paper memorized by now. I saw him when I arrived."

"Interesting."

"Yeah. He gives me the creeps. I wondered if he was a cop."

"I don't think so."

Linda made a face. "I think he's been watching everyone who gets into the elevator. He nodded just slightly to someone not long ago, I think, but I didn't see who it was."

When Peggy went back to her office, she looked directly at the man, but he looked back at his newspaper as soon as he saw her.

One of the detectives called her into Mr. Tyler's office as soon as he saw her. He closed the door, walked over to the desk, and opened the bottom drawer. With his hand in the drawer he looked up at her and spoke. "Miss Hale, I'd like to know if you've ever seen this before." He brought his hand from the drawer. He was holding a handgun.

She backed away and gulped. "Heavens no."

"You didn't know your boss kept this .357 Magnum in his desk, in a drawer with a false bottom?"

"No, I had no idea there was a gun in this office. I also didn't know the desk had a drawer with a false bottom."

"Do you have a key to this desk?"

Peggy took a deep breath. "No, but Mr. Tyler's secretary told me this morning that there is a duplicate set of his keys in the safe."

"Will you call her in here, please?"

Lillian was less than thrilled to be interrupted.

She looked annoyed as she walked into Mr. Tyler's office—until she saw the gun the detective was holding. "Have you seen this before, Ms. Frye?"

Lillian gasped and then squared her shoulders indignantly. "Indeed I have not." She stared at the gun for a moment and then looked up at the detective. "And I am called Miss Frye, thank you, officer."

The detective smiled. "Of course you are, Miss Frye. I should have known. Did Mr. Tyler keep this file cabinet and his desk locked at all times?"

"I never checked on him," Lillian answered without hesitation. "I was not authorized to touch his desk or file cabinet. If they were locked, either his wife or his partner must have had keys, since they opened everything this morning long before anyone else arrived."

The man smiled again. He apparently found Lillian's self-righteousness amusing. "Will you be so kind as to get Mr. Tyler's duplicate set of keys from the safe," the detective requested as he laid the gun down on the desk.

She glanced at Peggy and then nodded at the man. "Of course, if you wish." She spun around and marched out of the office to the safe.

Peggy felt apologetic. "Don't mind Lillian. She's known Mr. Tyler a very long time. She's just upset about his death."

When Lillian returned, the officer took the keys from her. "I'm going to lock up everything here. I'll take these keys and this gun to the lab. I'll give you a receipt for them."

Nick picked Peggy up before twelve for lunch. On their way to a restaurant, Nick nodded to the rearview mirror. "Your friends have stayed with me and they're staying with us. I don't think they like the company I keep. I went to see a friend at the Oceanside police station who's on limited duty, thus doing office work. Your friends parked down the street when I went into the station. Then I went to the cleaner's, the drugstore, the grocery store, and my apartment. I've given them a thrilling morning. I got their license number, and I'll call it in to Bob Watson. It'll be interesting to find out who they are."

"They're hardly my friends, whoever they are. It may be a rented car." She narrowed her eyes. "If I were going to tail someone, I wouldn't use my own car."

"Spoilsport. They still have to use their driver's license to get a rented car. What do you know about tailing someone?"

She tossed him a haughty look. "Absolutely nothing."

"Okay, tell me about your morning."

"You'd better wait until we sit down. It's been eventful."

Again she questioned her judgment about telling him everything, but after they were seated in the restaurant, she gave Nick a detailed report of her morning. He was thoughtful. "Well?" she asked.

"It's pretty interesting that Mrs. Tyler rented that car and Tyler had that gun and all those bankbooks."

"You know," she said, thinking aloud, "it seems a little dumb of Mr. Tyler to leave those bankbooks in his desk. Maybe his wife doesn't know about them. It just doesn't seem it would be in the normal scheme of things for him to close out that many accounts, with that much money, in such a short time. If he was doing something illegal or if he was going to take off. . . ."

"For instance, to a foreign country?"

"I guess that's what I'm thinking, but. . . ." She shrugged. "He could have been investing in another business or buying stock." She made a face. "I don't even know what I'm thinking about. If it was something like that, maybe he used a bank transfer or at least cashier's checks. Those accounts added up to an awful lot of money."

"It's your scenario."

"Yeah. I wonder how he did withdraw that money. I think you have to give a reason for a transaction over ten thousand dollars." She shrugged again. She was rambling, and she wasn't sure where her thoughts were leading. "One thing is certain, though: Someone thinks I've got two hundred fifty thousand dollars. I wonder if that's part of the money from those accounts. If so, where's the rest of the money?"

"Good question. Tell me, what do you think of his brother?"

Peggy shrugged. "No opinion. He didn't say much. He's older and better looking than Mr. Tyler."

He grinned. "You would notice that." He studied his coffee cup for a minute. "I'm interested in that man in your hallway."

"I checked with the police, and he's not a cop. I walked out to the hallway with the detective, but the man was nowhere in sight. I have a feeling he may have seen us coming and decided to disappear."

Nick scowled. "When we pulled away for lunch, I thought there was more than one car following us."

"Really?"

"Yeah. It's a black car."

"The car that followed you this morning was black."

"Yes, but that's a big year-old Ford. The other car is a foreign car, Japanese probably, much smaller and older."

Peggy took in her breath and told him about the car that seemed to be following her when she went to meet Scott. "I wonder if it's the same one? It was a small black car."

"Good question. Why didn't you tell me about it before?"

"Well, I'm still not sure he was following me. I don't usually pay particular attention to cars around me. I noticed that car only because I passed the restaurant and had to make a U-turn. He made the turn also, and I remembered there'd been a similar car behind me most of the time since I'd left home."

Nick remained quiet on their way to his car, and when he got in he made an announcement. "I'm going into your office with you. I want to see this newspaper reader. If he's still there when I pick you up this afternoon, I'll have a little chat with him." He started the engine and looked over at her. "Do you think you could get away about two?"

"No problem. I've nearly had it for today, but there are still a couple of things I want to do."

The streets were crowded with noon traffic when they left the restaurant, and although Nick was able to keep the big black car in view in his rearview mirror, he didn't see the smaller black car again. When they returned to the offices of Tyler Advertising, the little man was not in the hallway. Nick stayed only a few minutes, and then Peggy walked with him to the glass front doors of the reception area. The man was there, just down the hall. Nick nodded to him just before he got into the elevator. The man solemnly returned his nod.

When Peggy turned around, everyone was looking at her. Nick, of course, had been the point of interest. Her love life had long been a topic of undue interest to the staff of Tyler Advertising. She knew she inspired the curiosity by refusing to discuss her social life with anyone. Of course, no one believed it was nonexistent, and most thought she was merely being secretive.

She smiled at everyone and went back to her office, feeling a bit smug. She had no sooner sat down than the phone rang. "Peggy, who was that hunk who brought you back from lunch?"

Peggy laughed. "You should spend more time in the country, Linda."

"You mean you found him up there among all those trees?"

She decided not to tell Linda how accurate her statement was. "I'll tell you about it sometime. Don't get excited. He's just a friend."

"If I had a friend like that, I'd work for more."

"You sound like my mother." Peggy hung up and chuckled. Between Linda and her mother, she couldn't forget she wasn't involved with a man. She frowned at her desk. She hadn't heard from her mother. Apparently her parents hadn't heard about the murder. If only they would stay away until the whole thing was cleared up, she prayed silently.

She glanced out into the main office and was surprised to see Randall Barker heading her way. For just a flashing moment she wondered if he was as mystified by all that had happened as he appeared to be—or if he just happened to be a darn good actor.

Chapter Five

Randall walked directly to Peggy's desk, hitched his leg over the corner of it, and sat down. "I escaped." A smile played around the corners of his mouth. "Jennifer can be difficult at times. I've left her with Stan at the police station."

Peggy wanted to ask a lot of questions but decided on the polite one. "Is she all right?"

He laughed lightly. "Mad as a wet hen, of course, but she's okay. They're waiting for the woman from the car-rental agency. I think I believe Jennifer when she says she didn't rent that red car. There's something strange about that. What's been going on here?"

She hardly knew where to start, especially since she wasn't sure he wasn't somehow involved in all this. But he probably could get all the information from the police, so she told him everything. When she mentioned the bankbooks and the amounts of money involved, the unflappable Randall seemed on the verge of a coronary. "Are you all right, Randall?"

He let out a long breath. "Good grief! I can't fathom any of this. You know, I've known the Tylers a long time, but I've never known them well personally. We've never traveled in the same circles nor have we been very sociable except at affairs we were both expected to attend. I know they've always lived very well indeed."

He frowned at his shoes and then looked up at her. "For a long time now, Fred's been complaining to me that Jennifer was breaking him with her extravagance. I didn't tell her about it, but she was just telling Stan and me how Fred had been on her case for months telling her they'd have to economize. He told her they were heavily in debt." He frowned and appeared to be talking more to himself than to her.

Peggy cleared her throat. "Well, they're not alone, I guess." She wasn't sure he'd heard her. She looked up at him, but he was looking out the window at the clear blue sky. A good-looking man, he bordered on handsome, with his jet-black hair just barely touched with gray and a well-shaped mustache. *Why am I doubting him?* she wondered. Then she thought of Jennifer Tyler's face with its undeniable beauty. Randall and Jennifer Tyler would make a good-looking couple.

Mr. Tyler had not scored high in the good looks department. He was younger than Randall but didn't look it. He had pale skin, thinning blond hair, and small eyes behind dark-rimmed glasses. He was a man who had become soft and paunchy in the last few years, while Randall looked as though he spent a lot of time in a gym and a tanning salon. What did that mean, she wondered. Not much, probably. Though the office gossip about Jennifer Tyler ran rampant, as far as Peggy knew there had never been a word connecting the woman to Randall.

Suddenly he jumped to his feet. "I'll be in accounting if you want me. I'm not sure what I'll find, but maybe it's time I found out what goes on around here. You know, I've left the money-handling end of this business entirely up to Fred. That may have been the biggest mistake of my life." She heard anger in his voice for the first time since she'd met him.

Peggy watched him take long, determined strides across the art department and burst through the door of the accounting department. She would have liked to ask him about Mr. Tyler's brother. Then it occurred to her that there was another possible source of information about the man. She walked casually into Lillian's office. "Lillian, do you know Mr. Tyler's brother very well?"

Lillian gave an exaggerated sigh. "Not for years. I'm not sure what he's doing here. The two brothers have been bitter enemies. As far as I know, they haven't spoken in many, many years."

Peggy went back to her desk and looked over the notes she had made from the letters in Mr. Tyler's file. She placed the sheet of paper in her pocketbook. She hadn't decided just what she'd do with them yet or what she'd accomplish by doing anything. She took care of only the necessary work for that day and was ready to leave when Nick arrived. He was grinning like the proverbial Cheshire cat when he walked into her office. She looked up at him and raised her eyebrows. "Enjoying your vacation, are you?" she asked.

"More than I ever imagined." He placed his forearms down on her desk and moved his face close to hers. The proximity was a little unnerving, but she liked it. "I just shook up the newspaper reader in the hall," he said. His expression showed how much he had enjoyed it. "I opened the door to your reception area and yelled at the woman at the desk. I asked her if Peggy Hale had left yet." He grinned mischievously. "The woman flinched, but the little man lowered his newspaper and looked over it. Of course, the woman said no. I said, 'She has?' and then I stepped in and closed the door. Your receptionist thinks I'm bananas, but the little man was folding his paper when I glanced back. I'd like to have waited to see what he did, but I couldn't without his seeing me. His reaction proves to me, however, that it is you he's concerned about."

"Marvelous," she said without enthusiasm as she reached for her bag.

"Yeah. Look, if we want to get up to Bob's by four, we have to get rolling."

Peggy called Randall and told him she was

leaving. Then she stood up. "Let's blow this joint."

Nick laughed. "Great idea. We can't let our entourage get bored."

In the parking lot, the little man from the hall was looking at Nick's car. He saw them coming and scooted away. When they reached Nick's car, the man was standing several cars away watching them. Nick gave him a salute just before he climbed into the car.

Peggy had to laugh. "I don't think you made his day. Who do you suppose he is?"

"I have no idea, but if he follows us up to Mt. Laguna, I'll ask Bob to find out."

"Are you a detective for TLM?"

"Nope, nothing so intriguing. I design shopping centers, big office buildings, planned developments, and stuff like that." He grinned.

It occurred to her that he saw humor in many things and smiled a lot. She liked that. As she thought of it, she realized she liked *him* a lot too. He was a comfortable man, easy to be with, and good company. He had the one trait she liked most about people and rarely found in the opposite sex: He didn't take himself seriously. She'd have to be careful. It usually took her a long time to decide if she liked someone. One of her big flaws, she'd been told. She thought about his occupation. "So you have a creative mind and can dream up places for the rest of us to occupy in one way or another," she said.

"Yep. As long as it can be set in concrete, I'm supposed to be able to think of it and figure out how to do it."

She glanced over at him, but quickly looked away when she saw he was watching her while he started his car. They drove by the big black Ford. Nick signaled to the occupants that he was taking the west driveway out.

Peggy burst out laughing. "I can't believe you did that."

"Since we aren't going anywhere that will fascinate them, we may as well make it easy for them."

"You're crazy, do you know that?"

He glanced over at her while he waited for the traffic. "I don't think you mind."

She hit his arm playfully. "They could be dangerous men." He shrugged as he pulled out into the traffic. "You know, Nick," she went on, "you don't have to go up to Mt. Laguna with me. I can easily drive up there myself. I feel bad that I got you involved in all this. I also feel a little guilty that your vacation is being taken up with me." She really wasn't sure how she felt about that last part. She couldn't deny she felt a bit more secure in his company, but she certainly didn't *need* him with her.

He glanced over at her and his expression changed. The smile left his lips, but there was still amusement in his eyes. He picked up her hand and squeezed it while he waited for the red light to turn. "Being involved in 'all this,' as you call it, is a lot more exciting than listening to my beard grow. And I don't feel bad spending my time off with you. In fact, I've enjoyed every minute of it since you stopped trying to hit me with that attaché case."

Peggy fought a smile, unsuccessfully. She wasn't ready to admit how much she liked his company. He squeezed her hand again, and she squeezed his in return. That probably told him more than she wanted it to, she decided.

When they got out of his car in the parking lot of her apartment building, there was no sign of the men who had been tailing them. They were almost to the apartment-house door when Stan Tyler called to her. "Miss Hale, may I talk to you for a minute?"

He walked toward them, holding his body stiffly. Scott stepped from behind a car and followed his father. Peggy eyed the two men for a moment before she nodded. "Of course, Mr. Tyler," she said hesitantly.

"I have a few questions I'd like to ask you. Is there some place we can sit down?"

She glanced at Nick and then looked back at Stan Tyler. "Of course. We can talk in my apartment." She introduced Nick to the two men and led the way into the building.

Stan Tyler struck Peggy as being a totally different man from his brother. He was very soft-spoken and he appeared ill at ease. Both traits would have been totally out of character for his blustering brother. Scott sat down on the couch; Stan took a chair and sat straight, touching his neck brace.

"Miss Hale, I wonder if you'd mind telling me just what happened up at that cabin the night my brother was killed," Stan said. "My sister-in-law is quite irrational, which is understandable, I guess. Listening to her version, it's hard to tell what is fact and what is her own assumption. The sheriff gave me a sketchy report of what happened, but, as I said, I'd like to hear it from you. I know you answered some questions for Scott." He frowned as though troubled by a pain. "Fred and I were far from close, but he was my brother."

Peggy nodded. "I understand." She started with Mr. Tyler's phone call, presumably from San Francisco, and went through it all. Nick, too, told all he knew about that night. She noticed that Nick watched Stan Tyler closely throughout their monologues. She also noticed that Scott and Nick often appeared to be studying each other.

After they finished, Stan Tyler was thoughtful for a moment. He looked at Peggy and frowned. "You haven't remembered anything more about the man who shot at you?"

She shook her head.

"You didn't see anything inside the cabin at all?"

"No. It was after seven, the sky was heavily

clouded over, and it was starting to rain. The sheriff's deputy flashed his light inside before we left, but nothing looked unusual then. I guess the place was torn apart after we left."

He pressed his lips together and frowned for a moment. "You had no idea what was in the attaché case?"

Peggy let out a long breath. She'd been over this so many times it was becoming boring. "I thought it contained the Calloway files. I'll admit I thought it was heavy for that, but I didn't question what I'd been told. I just took it up there as I was asked to do."

"Do you know how long it had been in the safe?"

She frowned, wondering why he cared. "Lillian Frye said Mr. Tyler put it there the night before he left for San Francisco. I hadn't seen it there, but I rarely have reason to go to the safe."

Again he was thoughtful for a moment. He was beginning to make Peggy nervous. Scott's total silence was a little unnerving also. And it was getting late. Stan cleared his throat. "Do you know if there are spare keys to the attaché case, Miss Hale?"

She told him about the set of keys that had been in the safe. "The police have them now." She spoke crisply. A touch of anger was flaring up, and she worked to control it. She didn't tell him about the things that were found in his brother's office. She waited for him to ask about the money the detective had alluded to in the office that morning, but he didn't mention it.

Finally Stan stood up gingerly, holding the upper part of his body very erect. "I want to thank you, Miss Hale. You've been very informative." He looked over at Nick. "You too, Mr. Donovan." He looked at Scott. "Come on, Scott."

Scott stood up slowly and winked at Peggy. He spoke softly. "Thanks. He'll sleep better tonight." Stan left quite abruptly, she thought, with Scott sauntering along behind him.

Peggy closed the door and leaned against it. She looked up at Nick. "What do you think of them?"

Nick frowned. "I think there's something phony about that Stan Tyler. He wanted to hear your story all right, but I'm wondering why. It's doubtful either of us gave him any news. He seemed very interested in what you saw in the cabin and what you remember about the man who shot at you. He stared at you as you talked, as though he was studying you. I didn't like it."

"I didn't notice that, but I don't like his eyes. They give me the creeps. They're like bits of green ice, and I felt as though he looked right through me a couple of times. Do you think he's involved, somehow?" That was a new thought.

Nick shrugged. "I can't imagine how, but it's something to think about. Watch out for him. I doubt he's as shy and retiring as he appears.

Think back. Could he have been the man who shot at you?"

She let out a long breath. "Oh, Nick, I don't know. Like I've said over and over, I didn't really see him. It could have been anyone." She glanced at him playfully. "Even you."

She meant it as a joke, but he snapped back at her. "Come on, Peggy. . . ."

"I was kidding, Nick. It could have been anyone who has a bulky build or wore a bulky coat. By the way, what do you think of Scott?"

He slouched down on the couch. "Not much."

Peggy giggled silently as she picked up her bag. "He's quite good-looking, don't you think?" She didn't give him a chance to answer. "I'm going to change." She stopped at the door to her room. "You know, in Stan Tyler's place, I think I'd have asked what happened with the police after he left the office this morning. I wonder if he knows."

Nick narrowed his eyes. "You told Randall. Maybe Randall called him and told him. They could be in on this together, you know." He grinned. "Go change. If we're going to play Nick and Nora Charles, we'd better get to the scene of the crime."

"Yeah, I'll be only a minute. Guess you're an old-movie buff too."

He nodded. "You bet."

"Well, you can't be all bad. You know, we

might have trouble being Nick and Nora. We don't have a dog." She walked into her room.

"We can fake it," he called after her.

Peggy took óff her jacket and remembered the phone numbers she'd written down. She returned to the living room. "I want to try these two phone numbers and see what I get." She started pushing buttons. Nick placed his ear near the phone.

The first number was answered by a woman. "Tyler residence," she said with a heavy accent.

Nick and Peggy looked at each other. "Is Stan there?" she asked in her most sophisticated voice.

"No, ma'am," the woman said. "Mr. Tyler is out of town. There's been a death in his family."

Peggy said she was sorry. "Is Mrs. Tyler there?" She had no idea what she'd say if a Mrs. Tyler answered.

The woman's voice became leery. "There is no Mrs. Tyler."

Peggy apologized and hung up. She looked at Nick. "Guess there's nothing wrong there. After all, they were brothers. Maybe Jennifer had reason to call Stan. I wonder what the reason might be."

"Where'd you get that number?"

She'd forgotten she hadn't told him. "I copied two numbers from the Tylers' home phone bills. This is the other one." She hit the buttons again.

"Tyler Investments," a young, cheerful voice said.

Again, Nick and Peggy looked at each other.

He grabbed the phone from her and spoke in a very authoritative voice. "Let me talk to Stan, please."

The young voice turned deferential. "I'm sorry, sir, but Mr. Tyler will be away from the office for a few days. There's been a death in his family."

Nick hung up, and they looked at each other. He broke the silence. "Now, that's interesting. How many of these calls were there?"

Peggy clucked her tongue. "A few each month, but they always had two women's names beside them. What do you think?"

"I don't know. But, as I said, it's interesting, especially since the brothers weren't close."

"Or even on speaking terms, according to Lillian. I doubt that Jennifer Tyler is a close friend of Stan's housekeeper. And his office. . . ." She was thinking as she spoke. "Maybe Jennifer has a friend in Stan's office. That would seem an odd coincidence, wouldn't it?"

Nick nodded. "Yeah. Maybe your Mr. Tyler had a spy up in his brother's office for some reason, and he called for updated information."

Peggy laughed at that. "That's a little cloak-and-dagger, I think. Besides, these calls were all made during the day from the Tyler house. Mr. Tyler wasn't home during the day," she said, disappearing into her bedroom.

She thought about the two brothers as she slipped into jeans and a bulky sweater. She shoved her feet into a pair of old boots and grabbed her shoulder bag. She started talking as she walked back into the living room. "Tomorrow I'll see if I can think of a reason to look at our office phone bills. Our office manager guards the accounting office and its files as though they're the crown jewels. I'd like to see if Mr. Tyler ever called his brother's home or office during the day."

When they turned off the freeway onto Sunrise Highway, the big black Ford that had been following them went straight ahead. Nick chuckled. "They probably guessed where we were going and have no desire to visit the sheriff's station. If the smaller black car followed us, I haven't been able to pick it out."

Lieutenant Watson listened closely as they relayed all the information about the men tailing them, the man with the newspaper, and the visit from Stan Tyler. He already knew what had been found in Mr. Tyler's office. When Peggy finished telling him about the telephone calls to Stan Tyler's home and office, he leaned forward and frowned. "Now listen, Peggy, we really do have methods of our own for this sort of thing."

"I know that, lieutenant, but tomorrow I'll get into the office files and—"

He put his hand up to stop her. "Please, promise me you won't help us anymore. We'll check your office files if we feel the need. If, in your normal routine, you come across something that you think may be pertinent, give it to the San Diego PD or us, but do not—repeat, do *not*—check into anything yourself. Do you understand? You are *not* to try to help us anymore."

She cleared her throat. She knew when she'd been chastised. Again he sounded like her father. She decided she wouldn't tell him about the names she'd copied from the letters Mr. Tyler had handwritten. She wasn't even sure what she was going to do with them, but it didn't seem advisable to mention the subject to the lieutenant. "Okay, lieutenant, if you say so. I won't try to help you anymore." She turned her head away from him and looked out the window at two men in the parking lot.

When she looked back at the lieutenant, his eyes were narrowed and his hand laid across his midsection. "My ulcer is trying to tell me something," he said slowly. "I think it doubts your last statement."

Peggy stood up and put the strap of her shoulder bag over her shoulder. "It's probably telling you it's hungry. I've always heard that ulcers have to be fed often and at regular intervals. Try buttermilk. It helps my father." She stepped away from her chair. "You did say we could go through the cabin, didn't you?"

The lieutenant stood up and shook his head. "Yes, I did. I'll go there with you."

Nick grabbed her elbow and ushered her outside.

The small cabin looked ominous and lonely among the trees under the darkening sky. Peggy rubbed her arms as shivers shot through her. Nick noticed and put his arm around her. That helped. She felt a certain reluctance to go in, and she stopped at the steps leading to the small porch. Part of her reaction, she knew, was because of what had happened there. Part of it was caused by the yellow ribbons that cordoned off the doors and windows from people with nose trouble. And then the tree branches clamored noisily in the wind, which had picked up considerably since they arrived.

The red car was gone. After he unlocked the door and flicked on the lights, the lieutenant let Peggy precede him into the cabin. The living room was a shambles, with furniture tipped over, pictures askew, and two broken lamps. She picked her way through the debris, looking everywhere for she knew not what. An acrid odor permeated the air. Right then her bravado disappeared, and she silently wondered just what she was doing there.

They had been in the cabin for only a few minutes when Mr. Kolby stuck his head in the door. The elderly man apologized for intruding but said he thought the lieutenant would like to know that a man had been there that morning. "I didn't see him clearly, but he parked in front of the house here, walked around the back, and was there maybe ten minutes before he walked back to his car and left. It was that fancy sports car that was up here the night of the murder, I think. I wouldn't swear to it, but it looked like it."

The lieutenant was thoughtful. Finally he nodded to Mr. Kolby. "Thanks, Mr. Kolby. I'd appreciate it if you'd let me know if you notice anything else going on over here."

Mr. Kolby smiled. "Like I told one of your boys, I'll be glad to. You know, I thought I'd seen someone go behind the house earlier, but I didn't see him again and there wasn't a car here then. He was tall, but he was too far away and too fast for me to recognize him. With only the three houses here on this street and the third house up at the corner used only in the summer, we don't often see anyone around we don't know."

No one said anything for a moment, but Peggy's mind buzzed. What kind of car was it, she wondered. Mr. Kolby assured the lieutenant he didn't know much about makes of cars anymore. It was a low car, he said, one with lots of chrome and a shiny metallic gray paint job. It might be a Porsche or a Jag or one of the cheaper imitators, she thought. Did anyone connected with this case have such a car? *Who says we know everyone connected with this case?* she asked herself. She shook her head. Some of her earlier spirit returned, and she decided to try to find out the kinds of cars everyone connected with the case had access to. How she'd do it, she wasn't sure, but she was confident she'd find a way.

Then she froze and had trouble breathing. She listened to Nick's voice for a moment before she let herself realize the paralyzing thought that had flashed into her mind: Nick drove one of Datsun's low sporty Z cars. It was silver.

Chapter Six

Peggy continued to stand there looking through the desk in the corner of the living room, but she tried to think of the types of cars driven by others connected with the case. Surely Mr. Kolby knew Nick's car. Surely he'd recognize Nick, even from a distance, wouldn't he? Maybe his eyesight wasn't that good. She closed her eyes in an effort to clear her mind of those thoughts. Jennifer drove a black Mercedes, Randall had that red car, and Mr. Tyler had driven a white Cadillac. That much she knew. Scott had driven the black Mercedes to meet her. She wondered what kind of a car Stan Tyler drove. Probably the lieutenant knew. After Mr. Kolby left, she worked up the courage to ask him. She tried to make the question sound like idle curiosity.

His tone said he knew better. "Peggy. . . ."

"I just asked."

He let out a long breath. "Okay. He flew down from LA and rented a maroon Ford at the airport. He hurt his neck in an auto accident, remember? He says his own car is in the garage being repaired and he's not driving any more than he has to because it's quite painful for him to move his neck. He's not driving a gray sports car." He was agitated, she could tell.

She sighed dramatically. "I guess it wouldn't prove anything if he did drive a gray sports car. Nick drives one, and we can hardly call him a suspect." She said it casually and didn't look at the men, but she felt her chest tighten as she waited for a comment.

The lieutenant laughed. "I guess I'm Nick's alibi for part of Friday night, anyway. He had dinner with me at the diner down the road between about six-thirty and seven-thirty. He'd just gotten home when he heard the gunshots and found you running through the woods."

She glanced at the lieutenant, who was headed for the master bedroom. Nick had been going through some books, but he stood by the bookcase, watching her. She swallowed nervously. She hadn't meant her comment to be an accusation. Why was he looking at her like that?

She had been going through some papers while they talked. She picked up a piece of paper that had deep creases in it, as though it had been folded for a long time. It was also quite limp and dirty. She opened it and found a list of names with all but one crossed out. The last three names were Homer, Ben, and Tom. Only the name Tom wasn't crossed off. From Mr. Tyler's file she had copied down the names of Homer T. Castleberry, J. Bently Ashton, and Thomas Wylie. She folded the sheet of paper and replaced it. There wasn't anything concrete she could tell the lieutenant about it, so she decided not to mention it.

Next, she walked into the bedroom. Nick and the lieutenant were talking in the small bedroom where Mr. Tyler had been found. Everything in the room was topsy-turvy. She stooped down and picked up a woman's scarf that was lying on the floor. She put it to her nose and looked up at the lieutenant's frown. "Lieutenant, smell this."

He put it to his nose and raised his eyebrows. "Perfume, I guess. So what? It's a woman's scarf."

The scarf was made of fine silk and was emerald green, Jennifer Tyler's favorite color. "Did Jennifer Tyler come into the cabin Saturday?" she asked.

She had the lieutenant's attention. "No, she didn't. We wouldn't let her in until we'd checked through the place, but she said she didn't want to go in anyway. She hadn't been here since August, she said."

Peggy smelled the scarf again. "Lieutenant, this scarf has not been here since August. The scent of the perfume is much too distinct. I couldn't begin to guess what it might be, but I do know that when perfume lingers on a fabric for any length of time, the odor fades. Stale perfume is easy to detect. I don't believe this scarf has been here more than a few days."

The lieutenant took the scarf from her and said nothing.

She hesitated, not sure how much her opinion would be appreciated. "One thing doesn't fit, though."

The lieutenant looked at her and he wasn't frowning. "Oh? What's that, Peggy?"

She guessed she was back in his good graces. "I don't know what kind of perfume Mrs. Tyler wears, but I'd expect her to wear a more subtle and expensive scent than I think is on that scarf. Whoever wore this scarf likes strong flowery scents." Peggy went on looking through the drawers but found nothing out of the ordinary. She checked around the larger of the two bedrooms but found nothing unusual.

Nick went outside. Only a few minutes later, he called to the lieutenant through the front door. "Bob, they're calling you on your car radio." Peggy watched the lieutenant hurry out the front door, then she went out the back door. She wasn't sure what she hoped to find.

Nick joined her. "Find anything else that may make me look guilty?"

She shot him a glance. "Nick. . . ."

He shrugged. "Well, a couple of your remarks seem to indicate you think there could be a shadow of a doubt around me."

She stopped and turned toward him. "Nick, stop it. Stop it this minute." Her temper was close to the surface. "When I said it could have been anyone who shot at me, even you, I was teasing. Apparently you can't take a joke. When

I mentioned a few minutes ago that you had a gray sports car, I was merely making the point that because someone owned a gray car, it didn't mean he was involved in the murder." That was almost true. She narrowed her eyes at him and turned away, picking her way over a dead branch. "I'm not sure what I hope to find out here, but I'd like to look around, if it's okay with you, that is."

He didn't miss the sarcasm. "You have my permission." His voice, too, carried sarcasm. "It's getting dark. The light on the back porch doesn't shine far. Watch your step." He turned and walked back toward the front of the house.

She watched him go and let out a long breath. "Men!" she said out loud. "Their egos are so delicate." She kicked a small branch and edged her way to the rim of the light. Looking off into the darkness, she relived her recent flight through the trees. After her eyes adjusted to the darkness, everything became easier to discern. Something moved. She didn't. She only stared into the darkness.

It seemed an eternity before she saw the movement again. And then a figure bolted from behind a large tree and started to run. Peggy yelled to Nick and started running after the figure. She didn't want to lose sight of the fugitive. She was a lot more surefooted than she had been in the rain Friday night, and she wasn't nearly as frightened.

The tall figure continued to run, ducking in and out of the trees, but Peggy felt she was gaining on the person. When she realized Nick wasn't behind her, she yelled to him again. And then she screamed. Just then, the figure ahead of her turned to look back, stumbled, and after just a few more staggering steps, fell to the ground. Peggy wasn't sure what she could do to hold him. She wasn't even sure she should approach him. Moving toward the body lying on the ground, she picked up a fallen branch, hoping it might be of some help in protecting her.

Her spirits rose when she heard Nick and the lieutenant calling to her as their running footsteps raced through the underbrush in her direction. "I'm over here," she yelled at the top of her lungs as she placed her booted foot on the back of the prone body while she held the branch back over her shoulder. She had a good grip on it with both hands. She prayed that whoever it was wouldn't move.

When the body on the ground did move slightly, Peggy sucked in her breath. It was a woman, a young woman, and she was crying. Before Peggy could say anything, Nick and the lieutenant came up beside her. "Leslie," Nick said in a shocked voice, "what are you doing here?" He reached down and helped her to her feet.

Peggy looked from one to the other. "You know her?"

"Yeah, I know her all right. Her name is Leslie

Adams. Her folks have a cabin over beyond ours. The lieutenant knows her only too well too." He looked up at the lieutenant.

The tall man nodded, and Peggy thought she could see a smile playing around his lips. "Indeed I do," he said softly.

Nick took Leslie's arm and turned her around. "Come on, let's go into the house."

When they stepped into the kitchen of the cabin, Peggy looked Leslie Adams up and down. She was a tall woman with a model-thin figure and long brown crimped hair that was starting to escape from a bun at the nape of her neck. She appeared to be in her middle twenties. There was something about her that made Peggy clench her teeth, but she couldn't have said what it was. Nick picked up an overturned chair and sat Leslie down rather roughly. The lieutenant said nothing, and Nick was anything but friendly to her. "Okay, Leslie, what were you doing out there?"

"Oh, Nick. . . ." She started to cry again.

Nick didn't buy it. "Knock off the tears, Leslie. Don't forget, I've known you most of your life. You've always turned the tears off and on at will. What were you doing out there? Why did you run?"

She gulped a time or two and then spoke in a weak voice. "I was afraid, Nick."

The lieutenant's lips twitched in a repressed grin. "Leslie," he said, allowing a thoughtful pause, "you haven't been afraid of anything since you started walking." He looked down at her and his voice became authoritative. "This isn't just another traffic ticket or another complaint about a wild, loud party. There's been a murder in this cabin. If you have any information, I suggest you tell me."

She burst into tears again. "Oh, yes, poor Freddie. . . ."

"Freddie?" Peggy asked, her eyebrows high on her forehead. She'd never heard him called that by anyone.

After much gulping and sniffling, Leslie started talking. She claimed she and Freddie had been in love for nearly a year.

"He was fifteen or twenty years older than you," Peggy blurted out, as though such things didn't happen every day. What shocked her more than the fact that Mr. Tyler had been having a romance was that it was with someone like Leslie. Knowing Jennifer Tyler, that was almost unfathomable.

Leslie swallowed nervously. "I know, but we were truly meant for each other." Somehow, Peggy kept from groaning.

The drama in her delivery of that line made Nick mad. "Come off it, Leslie."

She gave them a sad little smile and went on. "You all know his wife is a real witch."

The lieutenant dropped his eyelids. "Never mind the character analysis, Leslie."

She sighed. "Well, Freddie and I were going to run away. He told me about a little villa he was going to buy outside of Rio. He said he had enough money for us to live the good life down there for as long as we wanted to. Oh, we had some wonderful plans." She gulped again and looked around at them all. Now that she'd started talking she seemed willing to go on, but she wanted prodding.

Her audience waited, so Peggy gave her the encouragement she was waiting for. "Go on, Leslie," she said softly.

Leslie enjoyed being at center stage. She looked around at everyone with that sad smile again while she slowly pulled the pins from the bun and let her hair fall around her shoulders. She shook her head and ran her fingers through her hair. Peggy bit her tongue so she wouldn't yell at the woman. Leslie finally took a deep breath and went on:

"The last time I saw Freddie was last Sunday, a week ago yesterday. We went over all our plans. I was to meet him here at six o'clock sharp, Friday night. I was to leave my car at my folks' cabin and walk over through the woods. He said he had everything ready to go. We'd go into San Diego Friday night, stay at a hotel, and catch an eight o'clock flight to Rio Saturday morning. He had the tickets."

The lieutenant frowned. "What did you do Friday night at six o'clock?"

She swallowed deeply again. "I came over a little early. It must have been about five-thirty. I saw a gray sports car sitting in front of the house. I don't know what kind it was." She smiled vaguely at Nick. "It was a much more expensive one than yours, Nick, and newer. It was really snooty. Anyway, I waited out back. I wondered about that car, because I didn't see any lights on in the house. Also, Freddie had been so adamant that I not be late. He said we had to be out of here no later than six-fifteen. He didn't want to take a chance and be here any later. He didn't say why, but I thought maybe he felt his wife might come up." She shrugged.

Peggy couldn't believe how relieved she felt about Leslie's appraisal of the gray sports car. Of course Peggy had been sure it hadn't been Nick's but . . . really knowing still felt good.

Nick gave her a tight smile before he turned a chair around and sat down opposite Leslie. "Okay, Leslie, go ahead," he said in a normal voice. He had calmed down.

Leslie took a deep breath. "I waited a little while. Then I left my suitcase beside the house and went back to my folks' cabin. At about seven-thirty I returned. There was a tan car in front of the house, and I saw a woman banging on the door. I thought maybe it was his wife so I left in a hurry. Then I came back at nine. This time I came in my car. I was tired of running back and forth through the woods, and besides it had been raining. The tan car was still in front of the house." Her voice cracked, and Peggy wanted to scream. Leslie was playing this scene for all it was worth.

The lieutenant and Peggy glanced at each other, and then they looked back at Leslie. Nick glared at her. She played with a tissue in her hands for a moment and then she started talking again just in time. Peggy felt she only had about one more minute of patience left.

Leslie cleared her throat and went on slowly. "I pulled into the driveway of that house at the corner of the street because I knew those people weren't here. I waited awhile. About the time I decided to leave, a sheriff's car drove in. Then I saw Nick's car. I got down in the seat so Nick wouldn't see me. I stayed that way until Nick pulled up in front of this cabin. Then I sat up. I waited until you all left." She looked up at Peggy. "I guess the tan car belonged to you."

Peggy nodded. "Yes. That was probably me you saw banging on the door about seven-thirty."

"Did you see a man around or hear any gunshots?" the lieutenant asked.

She shook her head. "I didn't look around much. When I saw a woman knocking on the door, I just split as fast as I could."

That was understandable. "Okay, Leslie, about nine you were parked up in the driveway at the corner house when the sheriff's car and Nick and Peggy left. What did you do then?" the lieutenant asked. Peggy wanted to yank the information from her. Leslie kept pausing between her sentences and smiling at Nick. The woman was driving Peggy bananas.

"Then I came down to the cabin and knocked on the door and called, but got no answer," Leslie said finally. "The place was all locked up. I didn't know what to do." She gave Nick a rather pathetic look.

He gave her no comfort, if that was what she wanted. "Then what?" he asked sharply.

"Well, I saw the note Peggy left and couldn't understand it at all since it was addressed to Randall. Anyway, I retrieved my suitcase from the side of the house and I left Freddie a note. All I said was, 'I'm ready and waiting for you.'" She looked up at the lieutenant. "You didn't find my note?"

"No."

She shrugged. "Then I went back to my folks' cabin. I waited all night for him to come. I came over the next morning about six, but the sheriff's cars were here so I left. Later in the day, I learned of Freddie's death." The tears flooded out again. Peggy didn't believe even one of them was real.

"What are you doing here today?" the lieutenant asked.

Leslie smiled at the lieutenant and Nick. Peggy couldn't believe the innocent expression Leslie was able to put on her face. "I'll be honest," she said, looking the lieutenant directly in the eye.

She hesitated a moment, and Peggy wondered if it was possible for her to be honest. Leslie shrugged and continued, "I hoped to be able to get in this cabin and find those tickets Freddie had to Rio. He claimed he had them hidden with a lot of money here at the cabin in a real safe place. I came over earlier today, but I saw that gray sports car out front. I left. That was about midmorning." She shrugged her shoulders again. "Probably whoever killed him got the money and the tickets." She sounded petulant.

"Did you see the person who was here this morning?" the lieutenant asked.

"Well, it was a man, but there wasn't anything unusual about him, if that's what you mean. I figured his car was the same one I saw here Friday night, but I'm not sure."

"Did you see what he was doing?" the lieutenant asked.

"Not really. I kept out of sight. I think he just walked around the house. He left soon after I got here."

Peggy picked up the scarf the lieutenant had laid on the table. "Is this yours?"

Leslie frowned while she examined the scarf. "No, I wouldn't be caught dead in this shade of green or this perfume. It must belong to the witch."

Lieutenant Watson glanced at Nick and Peggy before he reached down and took Leslie's arm.

"Come on, Leslie, you'd better come down to the station with me."

"You know I'll call my father, lieutenant. He'll—"

The lieutenant didn't let her finish. "I'll call him for you, Leslie, if you'd like. You can tell him how I beat you into submission. Nick and Miss Hale will back you up, I'm sure, just as your friends did the last two times you pulled that." He grinned down at her as he let her precede him out the door. "You should have learned by now that as much as your father cares for you, he isn't stupid and there are things even he can't control. Also, everyone in the world isn't waiting to vouch for your lies."

Nick, who had led Peggy out the door ahead of the lieutenant and Leslie, looked back and laughed lightly. "For a smart girl, Les, you sure are a slow learner."

They had no sooner returned to the station than the lieutenant received a phone call. He listened for a moment, and then he looked over at Peggy. "Do you know if Mrs. Tyler was ever a blond?"

"Yes, she was, up until about a year ago." It had been a great shock to the staff when Mrs. Tyler's hair had become bright red.

He repeated her answer and listened for a few minutes more before he hung up the phone. "Mrs. Tyler wasn't the one who rented the red car, but her driver's license was used." He sat down.

"Oh?" Peggy asked, hoping he would continue.

He smiled at her open curiosity and let her stew in it for a minute before he went on. "That was Sergeant Burke. The woman from the car-rental agency couldn't identify Mrs. Tyler. She did, however, recognize her driver's license when it was shown to her. She said she loved the woman's long blond hair. She admitted she hadn't looked at the woman too closely, but she was sure Mrs. Tyler was not that woman. Sergeant Burke showed her a picture of Fred Tyler. She identified him as the man who was with the woman who rented the red Porsche. She said the woman was almost as tall as the man. Her face was thinner and her voice was different from Jennifer Tyler's. She didn't take off her sunglasses. The man appeared to be in a hurry and impatient."

"Mr. Tyler was always in a hurry and impatient," Peggy said. There went one of her suspects. She hadn't really taken time to figure out how, but in the back of her mind, she felt that Mrs. Tyler had to be involved in some way. "Mrs. Tyler is four or five inches shorter than Mr. Tyler." No one commented. She went on talking more to herself than to anyone else. "It looks like Mr. Tyler knew Randall had left the cabin. He wanted that red car out front so every-one would think Randall was still there."

Lieutenant Watson sat up and leaned forward on his desk. He wagged his forefinger at her. "Now, you just leave the suppositions to us, do you understand?"

"Yes, sir," she said crisply.

"By the way, the gun found in Tyler's desk is not the one that shot him." The expression on the lieutenant's face told her it was time to leave.

Peggy stood up and walked out of the office. Leslie Adams was sitting in the next office, smoking a cigarette and waiting for her statement to be taken. Peggy looked at her for a moment before she opened the door and walked in. "I have another question for you, Leslie."

Leslie almost laughed. "Oh, you do, do you? What makes you think I'll answer it?"

"Because it may be in your best interest, that's why." The expression on Leslie's face said that Peggy had at least gotten her attention.

The lieutenant and Nick stepped up behind Peggy. Nick picked up her hand and squeezed it. She spoke quickly, before anyone could stop her. "Leslie, were you the one with Mr. Tyler when that red car was rented?"

Leslie leaned forward. Her face became hard and her eyes flashed. Leslie had become a little cocky since she'd talked to her father on phone. She stared at Peggy for just a minute, and then she leaned back in her chair and grimaced.

"Okay, I was the one. So what? All I did was sign Jennifer Tyler's name to the papers. Big deal!" She glared at Peggy defiantly, as though daring her to make something of it. Then, suddenly, Leslie looked down at the floor and shrugged. When she looked back up, her expression suggested bored resignation. Peggy wondered if what Leslie had thought was a lark up at the cabin was beginning to worry her. Of course, she could have been just getting bored sitting in that office without anyone to pay attention to her.

"Do you know why Fred Tyler wanted that particular type of car?" the lieutenant asked.

Leslie looked up at him. "I don't have to answer."

The lieutenant shook his head. "No, you've been through this routine enough to know you don't have to answer any questions, Leslie."

She laughed lightly and put out her cigarette. "Why not? I haven't really done anything. Freddie took his wife's driver's license from her wallet for a day. He said he'd return it that night. He didn't think she'd miss it. Anyway, he said that with a blond wig and a bulky coat and a lot of makeup, I was a ringer for his wife the way she looked in the picture on her license. I'm taller, but he didn't expect the clerk at the rental agency to notice. I wore my flats and big sunglasses. He wanted that particular car so if it was seen, anyone would think it was his partner's. He didn't want anyone to know he'd been at the cabin that day. He only intended to pick up the tickets and the money he had stashed there."

Peggy jumped in before anyone else said anything. "Then Mrs. Tyler knew he wasn't in San Francisco." She looked from the lieutenant to Nick and then back at Leslie. "And a week ago Sunday wasn't the last time you saw him?"

Leslie shook her head and almost laughed. "Of course his wife knew he wasn't in San Francisco. He called me at home in San Diego early Friday morning and said he'd pick me up at ten. He knew my folks weren't home, and he knew I was going to call in sick to my office that day so I could get packed and get up to the cabin on time. We went to the rental agency. He'd already arranged for the car he wanted, by phone. I followed him to his house out on Point Loma and we left his Caddy. His wife was at the hairdresser, he said. Then he took me home. He said he had a few things to do. I don't know what they were. Anyway, I was supposed to meet him at the cabin at six o'clock that night. I've told you everything else." She lit another cigarette.

Peggy had one more question for her. "Leslie, what kind of a car do you drive?" A frown creased the lieutenant's brow but Peggy ignored it.

Leslie laughed out loud. "It's a three-year-old yellow Datsun with a dented fender. Anything else?"

*   *   *

The lieutenant herded Peggy and Nick out to the parking lot. Peggy wanted to ask him if he believed anything Leslie said, but she thought better of it. She brought up the obvious. "Neither Mr. nor Mrs. Tyler ever went to San Francisco, and she lied through her teeth about that."

"We'll talk to her about that," the lieutenant said.

Nick hadn't said much since they left the cabin, and Peggy sensed he wasn't in the best of moods. Surely Leslie had been part of it. Peggy wondered how much Nick believed Leslie, and she did plan to ask him as soon as they were alone. Even with all Leslie's tears and gulping and deep breaths, Peggy felt there was a touch of defiance just beneath the surface of Leslie Adams. After she admitted passing herself off as Jennifer Tyler, the defiance was no longer hidden. Peggy would be willing to bet that scarf was hers too, but she didn't want to push her luck with the lieutenant by mentioning it.

It was dark when they stepped outside, but at the curb, by the light of the sheriff's station, a small black car showed up clearly. In it a man hurriedly raised a newspaper in front of his face as they walked from the building.

Peggy tapped the lieutenant's arm. "I think the man in that car who's trying to read the newspaper in the dark is the one who was in the hall outside my office today. If he isn't, I think you should talk to him anyway. He's missing an oar if he thinks he can read the paper in this light."

Nick leaned forward and looked at the man in the car. "Yeah, Bob, she's right. I'd bet on it." He slipped his arm around her waist and squeezed it. She liked that.

The lieutenant hesitated just a moment while he studied the car. The man laid the paper aside and started the engine. Telling Peggy and Nick to stay put, Lieutenant Watson moved quickly and was at the driver's door of the car before the man had a chance to pull away. He talked to the man for a moment, and then the man shut off his engine and got out of the car. He took out his wallet and held it in front of him. Lieutenant Watson studied it and then called Peggy and Nick over to him. "Do either of you recognize this man?"

There was no doubt in Peggy's mind. "Yes, that's the man who hung around the hall outside my office today." She frowned at the man. "Why were you there?"

Lieutenant Watson frowned at her. He turned his attention to the small rumpled man. "Would you mind answering the lady's question?"

The man looked at Peggy for a moment, then at Nick, and then back at the lieutenant. He let out a long breath as he reached in his jacket pocket and brought out a little black leather card case. He held it open to the lieutenant and then to Peggy and Nick. His name was Joseph P.

Dixon. He was a private detective. Lieutenant Watson raised his eyebrows. "You're following Miss Hale?"

The man nodded.

"Why, for heaven's sake?" she shouted. Nick picked up her hand and squeezed it. The lieutenant frowned.

The man smiled thinly. "I don't even have to tell the police that, lady."

"Even when there's assault and battery and murder involved?" she shouted.

The man lowered his eyelids for a moment before he looked up at the lieutenant. "Murder?" Although he had given Peggy a disapproving look, Lieutenant Watson nodded but said nothing. "Look," Joe Dixon began slowly, "no one said anything to me about murder. This woman hired me and said she wanted to know every place Miss Hale went and everyone she saw. I thought it was funny that she stressed several times that she wanted to know every place she went. Finally she let me in on the reason. She claimed Miss Hale was fooling around with her husband. She wanted to know not only the times they met but where they met."

Peggy became incensed. "Is that what you do for a living?"

He shrugged. "Look, it's a living, lady. Something did seem a little flaky, but I don't question those who appear to be well-heeled clients." He looked at Lieutenant Watson. "Anyway, I haven't seen Miss Hale go anywhere except to her office and a little restaurant out at Point Loma. I haven't seen her with anyone except this fellow here and another young fellow the woman said wasn't her husband from the description." He drew in a deep breath. "I don't know anything about a murder." He wiped his brow and ran his fingers through his graying hair. "I did see a light-haired man with a brace on his neck and the fellow she met at Point Loma go into her apartment building with her and this man, but other than that, I haven't seen her with any other guy. I told my client that no more than an hour ago."

"When were you hired?" the lieutenant asked.

"Saturday afternoon."

"Who is the woman who hired you?" the lieutenant asked.

He screwed up his face and let out a long breath. "Okay, I can't afford to be mixed up in any murder. She said her name was Gallager. Janet Gallager. She didn't give me her address. Said her phone wasn't connected yet because she'd just moved into her place in La Jolla. She said she'd call me each night at midnight for a report. She gave me a thousand dollars in advance." He wiped his forehead again.

"Isn't it a bit unusual for a client to give you such a large retainer and to call you at midnight for a report?" the lieutenant asked.

"In this business, you meet all kinds. She

seemed okay. She suggested midnight calls because she figured Miss Hale probably wouldn't be going anywhere at that time of night and I'd be able to give her a good report. She's called me every night on my car phone and a few times during the day too."

Nick, who had said little since the man started talking, spoke up. "What does this Janet Gallager look like?"

The man clucked his tongue. "She's a looker, all right. She's about your height, Miss Hale, and has a great figure. She wore big sunglasses even though it was cloudy out last Saturday and my office isn't as bright as it could be. I can't say much except that she had good skin, wore a lot of makeup, and she smelled expensive. She wore a hat that covered most of her head, but I could see a few strands of red hair. She's an expensive one, I'd bet. You get so you can tell in this business. Isn't that right, lieutenant?"

The lieutenant didn't answer him. Instead he called to a deputy who was just getting out of a car. He looked down at Joseph P. Dixon. "I'm going to want a statement from you."

"Sure, you bet, lieutenant. Joseph P. Dixon is well known in San Diego for cooperating with the police."

After the deputy led Dixon into the building, Lieutenant Watson took Peggy's elbow and hurried her to Nick's car. He opened the door and gave her advice in a stern voice as she slid into the seat. "Remember, you are *not* to help us. We're here to help you." He looked over the roof of the car at Nick. "That goes for you too, Nick." When he looked back down at Peggy, his lips smiled slightly. "Be careful, Peggy. Let us know if you hear any more from those men who are after that money. I'm going to talk to Sergeant Burke about putting a tap on your phone."

Peggy shrugged. "Whatever is needed, lieutenant." She said a silent prayer that her mother would stay in Mexico. She could blush at the thought of a stranger listening in on her mother's calls. The topics of conversation her mother chose were always unpredictable and more varied than one could believe.

By the time they reached San Diego, Peggy was furious. By the time they reached her apartment, she was raving. She was so angry at Jennifer Tyler for putting a private detective on her trail, she wanted to scream—preferably at Jennifer Tyler. How dare she do such a thing? Of course, the reason she had given the detective was a lie. Her husband was already dead when she hired him.

"One thing we know," she told Nick as she put on a pot of coffee, "is that one way or another, that woman was involved in her husband's death and she knows about the missing money. Otherwise she wouldn't care where I went or whom I saw. And she wouldn't have lied about that San Francisco bit. I'm so furious, I could—"

Nick slipped his arms around her waist and pulled her close to him. Before she could protest, he dropped his lips to hers and held her so close she could hardly breathe. She wanted to protest, but slowly her fury ebbed and she pushed her hands up his arms until they encircled his neck. He raised his head just enough to look deeply into her eyes. He spoke softly. "I liked that a lot."

She watched his eyes sparkle for a moment and then she lowered her own. "Ummm, me too." No sense denying it, the man was no dummy.

"We'd better try it again to make sure it wasn't just a fluke." Before she could comment, he dropped his lips to hers again and pulled her so close she could hardly breathe. She cooperated fully, and it wasn't a matter of not having a choice.

Nick could not help but know how she felt about him. She had no idea if it surprised him, but it did surprise her. She hadn't really had time to put a lot of thought into her feelings for him, but she was more than aware of the effect he had on her. She had been trying to keep it in the back of her mind since she'd left him that first night she met him.

Well, now he also knew how she felt. At that moment, she didn't care. When he raised his head again, he didn't let her go. "You know, I do believe that was the start of something very important in our lives." His eyes smiled down at her. "What do you think, Peggy Sue?"

His words surprised her. But it was too late to try to bluff him. "You just may be right, Nickolas T."

He covered her lips with his again, and she didn't doubt for a minute that this was indeed the start of something very important in her life. Maybe she had met the man her mother had always told her about . . . the man who would set off little bells in her head when he touched her. Nick raised his head again and looked deeply into her eyes. Instead of bells, Peggy heard a brass band marching around inside her head. She barely heard the rapping on the door.

When she opened the door, Scott Tyler smiled down at her. "I've been calling you all afternoon. I was in the area, so I thought I'd take a chance and stop by to see if I could catch you."

She invited him in and closed the door. He nodded to Nick and turned around to face her. She cleared her throat. "I just got home," she said feebly, feeling uneasy without knowing why. The way Nick glared at Scott didn't help. She motioned to a chair. "Sit down, Scott. Coffee will be ready in a minute." She escaped to the kitchen.

She placed mugs and a plate of cookies on the kitchen table. She picked up the coffeepot, and when she turned around, both men were taking seats at the table.

"Peggy, I feel you are being treated rather shabbily," Scott began. "Jennifer has been way out of line accusing you. She talked to a reporter today and told him she knows you were in on her husband's murder and she intends to prove it. I criticized her for it and Dad did too. I know she's upset, but she went too far. We thought you should know about it. I don't think my father had any right to give you the third degree today, either." He smiled beautifully.

Peggy looked away from his big dark eyes. She sat down, still feeling uneasy. "I think your father just wanted to hear about it all from me. Do you have any idea what the initial problem between your father and his brother might have been?" That point had really been bothering her.

Scott shook his head and reached for a cookie.

"Watch your teeth," Nick said. "She keeps them in the freezer." Peggy frowned at him. He didn't have to say that.

Scott laughed lightly. "They do stay crisp that way, don't they?" He winked at Peggy, and she felt heat creeping up in her face. She nudged Nick's foot with her own.

"To answer your question, Peggy," Scott went on, "I don't really know what the problem was. Their feud came to a head when my grandfather died. It had to do with the old man's will. You probably realize there's about a ten-year age gap between my father and Fred."

"Yes, I did notice the age difference," Peggy said. She hoped he'd tell more.

"They had different mothers. From what I've gathered, Fred's mother was still alive when

Grandfather died, and she and Fred got more than a lion's share of whatever there was to inherit. I was just a kid at the time, and I've never really known the details. I think it was Uncle Fred's mother who created all the trouble between them. She didn't like my dad, didn't want him getting close to Uncle Fred. Maybe she was afraid he'd try to get some of their money." He laughed lightly. "It happened long ago and is hardly pertinent to anything now. Dad and I came down only because Jennifer was hysterical when she called Dad after the police notified her about Fred."

Peggy sipped her coffee. "Do you know Jennifer well?" She waited for his answer. Somebody called somebody at his father's house and office from the Tyler house quite often.

"I know her slightly. She's visited us a few times when she's been in LA alone." He looked at the cookie in his hand as he spoke. Peggy felt he was lying. She wondered why.

Scott finished his coffee and refused more. "I have to run. I guess I just wanted to apologize to you for my family, Peggy." He stood up. "I think I'll be around for a few more days. Dad and I want to do what we can for Jennifer. I'd like to take you to dinner, if I may." He flashed his disarming smile at Nick. "Of course, you'd be welcome too, Nick."

Nick pushed back his chair and gave Scott a look that said "no thanks" without words.

When Nick didn't say anything, Peggy spoke up. "The funeral is at nine tomorrow morning, isn't it?"

"Yes," Scott said as he walked toward the front door. "I'll call you later, Peggy." Peggy and Nick followed him. When Scott put his hand on the doorknob, he turned back toward them. "By the way, the police told us Fred was killed in the fight he had with someone rather than by the bullets he had in him. However, they say they don't know exactly what killed him yet. I can't believe they don't know if he had a heart attack or if he hit his head or what. I know you were up at the sheriff's office today." He smiled shyly. "I called your office, Peggy. Fred's secretary was kind enough to tell me where you were. I'm wondering if they've given you a clue to the exact cause of death."

Peggy took in her breath. "We know only that he died as a result of the fight." She thought she lied quite well. She sensed a tenseness in Nick, who was standing close beside her.

Scott shrugged. "I'll guess they'll tell us when they're ready. You know, the sergeant who was at your office this morning mentioned something about some money being involved. He refused to give us any more details beyond the fact that they had reason to believe Uncle Fred may have had a great deal of money on him. They won't say what makes them think that. Jennifer says the idea is preposterous. Have they mentioned anything about that to you?"

Peggy shook her head. "No, they haven't." Again, she thought she lied quite well.

When she closed the door behind Scott, Nick shoved his hands into the pockets of his pants. "He's a good-looking guy."

"I'm sure some think he's handsome." Peggy walked into the kitchen with Nick behind her.

"What do you think?" he asked as he carried their mugs to the sink.

"Oh, I think he's handsome, all right, but I think he came here on a fishing expedition. I'm wondering if he came on his own or if he was sent here by someone."

"He could be an errand boy for his father, or Jennifer Tyler, or even Randall Barker, I suppose."

Peggy put the cookies away in the freezer. "I think I've discounted Randall, but I'd vote for Jennifer Tyler. Since she obviously would have needed help, I'm voting for Scott's father. I think Scott may be being used. I may try to find out."

"What do you mean by that?" Nick turned her around to face him.

She was caught a little off balance. "I thought maybe I'd go out to dinner with him. Maybe I could learn something."

He took her in his arms and kissed her. When he raised his head he looked directly into her eyes. "I'll take you to dinner anytime and anyplace you want to go. I'll also teach you anything you want to learn."

She fought a grin. "You will, huh?"

"Yeah. Tell me there isn't anyone serious in your life."

"There's no one serious in my life," she said in a parrotlike fashion.

"Wrong! There *is* someone serious in your life, and don't you forget it. Remember, I told you we're starting on something very important here."

She had just enough time to say "Yeah" before he drew her tightly against him and caressed her lips with his.

When he raised his head, he smiled slightly. "How about that?"

She let out a breath. "Um, how about that?"

When Peggy went to bed that night, she tried to reignite her fury at Jennifer Tyler for having her followed by a private detective. Somehow, she had difficulty thinking of Jennifer Tyler at all. Her mind kept zipping back to Nick's embraces. She couldn't remember his exact words, as she wanted to, but she knew they had something to do with that kiss being the beginning of something. She didn't doubt he was right about that. She did wonder just what that something might be. She also wondered if they had the same "something" in mind.

She poked her pillow. She'd have to think

about all that later. First things first. Tomorrow morning, Mr. Tyler was going to be buried. Sometime after that, she planned to have a very long chat with Jennifer Tyler.

Chapter Seven

The phone rang while the alarm clock buzzed at seven o'clock the next morning. Peggy had put in a night of fitful sleep. She hit the button on her alarm and grabbed the receiver of the phone. When she answered, her voice was fuzzy, but she quickly became awake when the gravelly voice on the other end of the line spoke. "Miss Hale, our time is running out. We've determined the police aren't watching you, so we'll make our move today or tomorrow. Be prepared to hand the money over to us without any trouble and you'll come out of this all right. Give us any trouble at all and you'll have more than you can handle." The phone went dead.

Peggy stared at the receiver for a minute before everything registered. She immediately became angry. She slammed the phone down and got out of bed. As she marched into the shower, she worked on a speech she was going to give these jokers, whoever they were, the next time they called. She turned on the water and stood still for a minute. She swallowed hard. No matter how much she wanted to deny it, those phone calls frightened her. She was thankful that Nick was dedicated to making sure she wasn't alone. However, for a while that day, she needed to get away from him. She had things she wanted to check into, and she felt she'd get her best results alone. Closing her eyes, she thought, *When will this all end?*

Nick went to the funeral with her—for moral support, he said. His presence discouraged those from the office who might otherwise have wanted to cling to her or to gossip with her for firsthand information about the whole sordid ordeal. Among some of the city's more distinguished mourners were two men whose names she had copied from those handwritten letters in Mr. Tyler's files. She longed to talk to them about the letters, but of course the cemetery was not the place to do it.

J. Bently Ashton nodded as he moved in her direction. "Big loss, Peggy. To our community as well as your firm." He patted her arm and walked on to where Jennifer Tyler, with a black lace veil hiding her face, stood between her brother-in-law and Randall Barker. Scott Tyler stood behind her.

When Peggy looked up again, Homer T. Castleberry was walking toward her. His somber look matched J. Bently's, and he nodded as he came up beside her. "Very sad indeed, Peggy. We'll all miss him." He squeezed her arm, as he had done many times in the office, and walked on. He, too, spoke briefly to the grieving widow. Then Stan and Randall, with Scott close behind, turned Jennifer around and started her walking toward the undertaker's long black limo, which sat at the head of a line of long black limos.

Nick, who had said little since the services started at the grave site, squeezed her hand. "Good-sized crowd here. It's a little surprising. Tyler didn't have a reputation for being very friendly up in the mountains. He had that place up there for as long as I can remember, but not many people knew him."

Peggy looked around at the dispersing crowd. "I'll let you in on a secret. If you subtract the people who are clients of ours and their wives and Tyler Advertising employees, this service could have been held in a phone booth. It seems a little sad to me."

Nick continued to survey the group. "You must have an impressive client list. A lot of big names, with really big cars and flashy jewelry, are here."

"Don't let the well-known names and expensive cars fool you. In this age of easy credit and easy PR via local newspapers and television, it's not too difficult to get your name known and to come off appearing impressive."

Nick opened the door of his car and grinned down at her. "My, you have a cynical side to you, don't you?"

Peggy climbed into the car and returned his

grin. Maybe she had come off sounding a little jaded. When he got in behind the wheel, she laughed lightly, "I don't think I'm really cynical." She didn't like that image. "It's just that I know some of these people. They live the good life, spend money like water, and owe us and everybody else in town a fortune that will take forever to collect. Mr. Tyler did some PR work too, you know."

"No, I didn't know. He talked to me about his advertising business at times, but he never mentioned he did anything else."

Nick drove the short distance to the office building that held Tyler Advertising and found a parking space with not a little difficulty. He shut off his engine. "Do you ever do public relations work?"

She shook her head. "No, Mr. Tyler asked me if I wanted to help him out with it and do some copy, but I declined. I told him I work better with pictures and short, pithy phrases. Most of his PR clients were also our advertising clients. He did that kind of stuff by himself. He said he helped hide a lot of skeletons in closets by focusing attention on the front doors. I was never sure what he meant. One time Randall joked that the purpose of PR was to get your name in the news for the things you wanted to be known for, so that hopefully your goofs would be overlooked. Sometimes it backfires, though. Sometimes, well-known people get a lot of notoriety for things no one would notice if their name wasn't so well known. So much for fame, real and manufactured. I've got to run." She opened the door.

"When do you want me to pick you up?"

She really didn't want him to pick her up, but she didn't want to tell him that. She looked at her watch. It was eleven o'clock. "Why don't you call me about three? I'll let you know what's going on."

"What about lunch?" He leaned over and kissed her lightly.

She swallowed hard, fighting an urge to go for a kiss with more substance. Instead, she laid her hand on his and squeezed it. "I'll have someone bring me something to eat. I do that often. I've got a lot to do today." She jumped out of the car. If he knew what she wanted to do, he'd give her a lot of static about it and probably try to stop her. She hurried into the building before she turned to wave at him.

It wasn't easy for Peggy to be very friendly and confidential with anyone, even people she had known and liked for a long time. But pushing her natural instinct aside, she walked into Lillian Frye's office, perched on the corner of her desk, and, as though they were the closest of friends, she brought Lillian up-to-date on all that had happened since she'd left the office the day before. Well, almost all, anyway. Lillian absorbed everything with open fascination and hid what must have been the shock of Peggy's openness quite well.

When Peggy finished her monologue, she stood up, a little put off by Lillian's wide-eyed expression. However, Lillian, being Lillian, quickly reverted into the character everyone knew so well. "I told you that you shouldn't have been so quick to go up there last Friday. You've gotten yourself into all kinds of a mess because of it." She bobbed her head to show her righteous indignation.

Peggy let her eyelids drop and sighed. "I know now that you were right, Lillian."

Lillian frowned slightly and, for her, relaxed a little. "You know, I'm not surprised that the police were wrong when they accused Mrs. Tyler of renting that car. She's an odd one sometimes, but I couldn't see her doing that. She's always been pretty obvious with her shenanigans, but she's not dumb. That would have been dumb." She looked up at Peggy. "It does surprise me, though, that she hired a private detective to follow you. You weren't having a romance with Mr. Tyler, were you?"

"Really, Lillian!"

She shook her head. "I guess you wouldn't. You know, the gossips figure you have some clandestine romance going with someone, somewhere." She shrugged. "I'm sure you could do better than Fred Tyler, and I'm not sure you'd be his type, anyway."

"Thanks a lot, Lillian. By the way, you can discount the gossips. They are dead wrong." She paused. "Bad choice of words, under the circumstances. What did you mean, his type? Did Mr. Tyler have a type? I never thought of him as a . . . Don Juan."

Lillian almost smiled. "I don't mean to speak ill of the dead, but I guess the facts aren't really speaking ill. He was quite a lady's man, you know."

Peggy let out a long breath. "No, I didn't know. I will say that Jennifer Tyler and that Leslie Adams I met up at the cabin, who said she had been going to run away with him, are worlds apart."

"Ah, yes, he did diversify. I've known the man for years, and I'd have to say Mrs. Tyler was more his type, but he liked several types."

Peggy had never guessed what a gold mine of information Lillian could be once she got started talking. She felt pangs of guilt for purposely getting Lillian started, but she tried to digest all the information Lillian was now imparting. According to Lillian, Mr. Tyler had been quite wild in his twenties. Lillian had worked for Mr. Tyler's stepfather in those days. It was about the time the older man retired that Fred Tyler decided to go into business. "Fred was two years older than I was, but his stepfather insisted that I go to work for Fred in his new enterprise and give him all the benefits of my expertise."

As Lillian went on talking about Fred Tyler's three marriages, Peggy thought she detected a slight tone of jealousy she had never suspected before. "You know it's odd," Lillian went on, "that Jennifer Tyler would hire someone to follow you *after* her husband had been found dead."

Indeed. There were a few things Peggy hadn't told Lillian. The police still had not released the information about the phone calls she'd received about the missing money. They believed that by keeping the information out of the news, they were protecting her from other criminals who might do more than make phone calls. Also, Lieutenant Watson didn't want some joker to start digging up the property around the Tyler cabin looking for the missing loot. Peggy thought about telling Lillian, in the hope that she might know something, but she thought better of it.

Also, the police had said that Mr. Tyler died of injuries sustained during a struggle and not from the gunshots, but they had not said exactly what killed him. Peggy was very careful not to let anything slip, even though Lillian was a good inquisitor. It wasn't that Peggy harbored the slightest suspicion about Lillian Frye. It was just that Lillian might say something unknowingly to the wrong person. Peggy wished she had a clue about who that wrong person might be. Peggy also said as little about Nick as possible.

When Lillian finished her little dissertation about Fred Tyler, Peggy bit her lip. "Lillian, do you know which airlines Mr. Tyler used most of the time?"

She eyed Peggy for a long moment, and then a hint of a smile appeared on her lips. "One of the things you'd like to know is which airline he was booked on for Rio last Friday night and if the reservation was for one or two."

Peggy tried to keep a straight face, but couldn't stop her grin. "Yep." She wondered if she blushed. Lillian had seen right through her friendly pose. Peggy wanted to laugh out loud. Had she allowed gossip—and the fact that Lillian was so unlike anyone she had ever met before—to make her misjudge the woman for the last three years? She'd have to think about that later.

The hint of a smile on Lillian's mouth grew. "I'll see what I can find out. Anything else?"

Peggy almost giggled. Lillian was a different person. *Maybe I've chosen my confidante well, after all,* Peggy told herself. "Okay, Lillian, there is something else. Mr. Hanson guards the files in accounting as though they're Fort Knox. I'd like to see the phone bills for the company for the past year or so. I want to check on some LA calls from the office." She stood up to leave. "In fact, I'll get you the two numbers I want to check. I took them from the phone bills for the Tyler home."

Lillian nodded as she scribbled on her pad. "You want to know if anyone from here called Stan Tyler's home or office." Peggy frowned but Lillian didn't look up before she went on.

"They're the LA numbers called from the Tyler house most of the time even though they have women's names beside them. I doubt those numbers were ever called from here, except for the time a few years back when Mr. Tyler had me call the numbers to see who answered. Jennifer is the one who called them from the Tyler home. She wrote women's names next to them so her husband would think that they were the numbers of friends. Jennifer tried to get the brothers together about five or six years ago when Stan moved out here to the Coast. Fred was furious because she met with Stan then. I think that's why Stan opened his business in LA instead of San Diego. But obviously Jennifer has been in close touch with him." Lillian looked up and raised her eyebrows. "From the way they were acting yesterday, I'd say Jennifer and Stan have gotten to know each other very well through the years."

Peggy cleared her throat. "Maybe so. Where's Randall, do you know?"

"Yes, he's in accounting. Kept Hanson here until midnight last night. He went through every nook and cranny in this office and all the books. I don't know if he's on the trail of something or if he's still looking for a trail." She reached for her phone.

Peggy turned to leave but turned back.

"Lillian, do you know if Mr. Tyler had anything going with J. Bently Ashton or Homer

Castleberry or Thomas Wylie besides their account here at the agency?"

Lillian frowned. "No, not that I know about. Tom Wylie was J. Bently's accountant, but they had a falling out, I heard. I'm not sure Tom is working right now. I think Mr. Tyler's association with J. Bently and Homer Castleberry was strictly advertising."

"Thanks, Lillian. I'll check on that and see you later." Peggy walked into her office with more to think about than she had expected. She glanced at her phone messages and laid them aside. She wasn't sure why she felt it was crucial to find out the reason for the notes handwritten to those men, but the idea consumed her.

She called J. Bently Ashton's office first. She gave his secretary her name and waited only a few minutes before J. Bently picked up the phone. His voice was brisk. "Everything was finished with your boss, Peggy. Don't get any high-flown ideas that you can pick up where he left off. It's over and done with." He banged the receiver down. Peggy rubbed her ear.

She thought of calling him back and explaining her dilemma, but she didn't think he'd be receptive. She called Homer Castleberry, and if the words weren't exactly the same, the sentiment matched that of J. Bently's. Again, she wasn't given a chance to state her case. She wasn't sure where to reach Tom Wylie. Taking a chance, she called his home. He answered the phone. As soon

as she said who she was, he gasped. "Peggy, I
have to talk to you. Where can we meet? I. . . ."
The man was breathless.

Peggy cleared her throat. "I can meet you anywhere. Are you all right?" He didn't sound it.

"Yes, yes—at least, I will be if you can help
me." He gasped for air again before he gave her
the name of a coffee shop near her office. "Do you
know it?"

"I'll find it." The urgency in his voice excited
her. Maybe she'd really stumbled onto something. She grinned mischievously when she stuck
her head in Lillian's office. "If Randall's looking
for me, tell him I'll be back in an hour. I may
have hit on something. I'll let you know when
I get back."

"Oh?" Lillian said. "Something about one of
the three clowns?"

Peggy laughed lightly. "Maybe."

Tom Wylie was sitting in a booth wiping his
balding head with his handkerchief when Peggy
arrived. His face was flushed, his silver-rimmed
glasses were perched halfway down his nose, and
his shirt was unbuttoned at the neckline. The
man seemed on the verge of a heart attack. Peggy
slid into the booth, asked the waitress for coffee,
and looked at Tom Wylie closely. "Are you all
right?" she asked.

"Yes, yes, I'm all right. I just hope you can

help me out. I've got to get hold of that suitcase Fred had for me."

Peggy looked down at the table. "Tom . . . I'm afraid—"

He cut her off. "Look, he told me to be there at that cabin at nine o'clock on Friday night and I could have my papers and my money. He said you'd bring them up to him." It took him three matches to get his cigarette lit.

Peggy watched him. Mr. Tyler had told Leslie to be there at six, he had told her to be there at seven, and he told Tom Wylie to be there at nine. She idly wondered who might have had the eight o'clock slot. After Tom drew deeply on his cigarette, Peggy spoke softly. "Do go on, Tom."

"Well, I couldn't get away in time to make it up there by nine. My wife's brother and his wife arrived from out of town unexpectedly a little before six o'clock. You know how unexpected company throws a monkey wrench into your life. My wife just about became hysterical when I told her I had to go out. I finally got away from the house about nine and raced up to the cabin. When I arrived I thought both Fred and Randall were there, and I didn't want to go in because I didn't know how much Randall knew."

Peggy frowned. "You have no idea how confused I am. I thought Mr. Tyler was in San Francisco. Why did you think both Randall and Mr. Tyler were at the cabin?"

He took a deep breath. His nervous state appeared to be improving. "Fred Tyler told everyone he was going to San Francisco so he could clear up his affairs here. His wife went up to do some shopping. He told her he'd join her up there, but he didn't intend to. She thought as much and returned after spending one day there. He was planning to leave the country, but I doubt she knew that. Anyway, I thought both men were there because I saw their Porsches, Randall's red one and Fred's silver one, parked by the cabin."

Peggy gasped. "Mr. Tyler has—had a silver Porsche? I've only seen him drive a white Caddy."

A faint smile formed around Tom Wylie's lips while the waitress refilled their coffee cups. "Guess you don't know about his other life. No reason not to tell you now. He had a condo in the development not far from his home out on Point Loma. He kept his Porsche there. It was his pride and joy." He laughed nervously. "His wife didn't know about his other life, but he conducted his private business from that condo."

Peggy sipped her coffee, watching Tom Wylie over the rim of her cup. "What 'other' business did Mr. Tyler have?"

He laughed. "I can't believe you don't know. He trusted you more than most. That's why he asked you to take that attaché case up to the cabin. That's why I wanted to talk to you. I figured you'd know what happened to my money and papers. He had somebody staying at the condo, so we couldn't take care of our business there, but he told me everything would be in that attaché case. He said he'd leave it just inside the front door, if he had to leave. Peggy, your boss was a blackmailer."

Peggy took her time walking back to her office. She had a lot to think about. Mr. Wylie refused to go to the police with her right then, saying he had to explain it all to his wife first. He told her to tell the police and he'd back her up later. It wasn't the way she'd have preferred it, but it didn't seem she had a choice. She thought about trying to find Nick but decided against it without knowing why.

She'd rather tell the lieutenant about all this than Sergeant Burke, she decided. For one thing, she felt she knew the lieutenant better. Also, she couldn't help feeling a little smug about finding out some important information on her own.

According to Tom Wylie, by being involved with Fred Tyler, he was protecting himself and getting paid for it. While he worked as chief accountant for J. Bently Ashton, J. Bently's bank financed Homer Castleberry in the building of one of the largest developments of expensive homes ever attempted in San Diego County. There had been a great deal of creative bookkeeping done by both Ashton's bank and Castleberry's construction company. Tom Wylie had set up these creative maneuvers. He had been well paid for the deed. Somehow, Fred Tyler had learned about it.

To save his own neck, Tom Wylie supplied Fred Tyler with documented information about the embezzlement, which Fred Tyler in turn used to extort large amounts of money from the two firms. According to Tom Wylie, Ashton and Castleberry were not the only firms to be caught in Fred Tyler's web. Last Friday night, Fred Tyler was to leave the incriminating papers and a payoff of two hundred fifty thousand dollars in the attaché case for Tom Wylie at the cabin. Peggy had accused Tom of calling her about the missing money, but he'd denied it vehemently, and she believed him as he broke out into a sweat.

By the time she walked into her own office, Peggy had her plans more or less formed. She didn't intend to tell Randall or Lillian what she had learned, yet. It wasn't because she thought either of them was involved, but. . . . She'd also decided she'd better tell Sergeant Burke. She called his office, only to learn he would be tied up until after two at a presentation luncheon. She asked for Detective Lowe, who had searched Mr. Tyler's office, but he was out too. She hung up and decided to go with her other plan.

She called the sheriff's station at Mt. Laguna and was told that Lieutenant Watson was expected to be back in the office by two. It was a little after one. "Tell the lieutenant that Peggy Hale is on her way to see him." She smiled as she hung up. That would surely make his day. She called a cab, stuck her head into Lillian's office, and tried not to sound too excited. "If anyone is looking for me, tell them I had to go up to the sheriff's office at Mt. Laguna."

Lillian's eyebrows shot up. "Something interesting?"

"Not sure. I'll tell you later." She frowned. "If a man by the name of Nick Donovan calls. . . ."

"I'll make sure I get his call and that he knows where you are." She grinned more broadly than Peggy would have thought she could.

At her apartment building, Peggy's first instinct told her to get into her car and head for the mountains, but she was still in the clothes she'd worn to the funeral. She had a strong desire to change.

Just as she put her key into the door of her apartment, two men came up behind her. "Go inside and be very quiet, Miss Hale." Peggy gasped as she looked up at the two well-dressed men. One man grabbed her upper arm and squeezed it tightly. "Open that door, Miss Hale."

Just then the door across the hall opened. Peggy turned. "Hi, Mrs. Brady. Have you had any trouble with your lock? I'm having a terrible time getting this lock open." Peggy's breath came in short gasps, but if there was anyone in the building who had an answer to every problem in the world, it was Mrs. Brady.

Mrs. Brady walked toward them. "No, I haven't, Peggy. Let me see if I can get it. Sometimes you just need to give it a certain twist." She took the key from Peggy's hand and gave the lock a jerk. "There you are," she said with satisfaction. "You just have to hold the knob the right way. I just saw our new maintenance man out front. I'll make sure he checks it before he leaves." She nodded to the two men and left.

One of the men narrowed his eyes. "Very cute, Miss Hale, very cute. Now, let's go inside. We have a lot of money to talk about." He pushed her none too gently.

Chapter Eight

Peggy stumbled inside. If she wasn't ever seen again, at least Mrs. Brady had seen these two men. They had no more than closed the door when there was a loud knock. "Miss Hale, it's Morris Everett, the new maintenance man. Mrs. Brady says you're having trouble with your lock."

Peggy smiled at the two men and opened the door. "Yes, Mr. Everett, this lock sticks or something every once in a while. Here's my key." She stood back and watched the man fool with the lock that had always worked perfectly well.

He tried it several times and shrugged. "It seems to be working okay now. Maybe it's just temperamental." He laughed lightly. "I think we should put a new one in. I'd hate to have you get stuck in the hall some evening and not be able to get in." He looked up at the three of them and smiled.

Peggy nodded. "Maybe that would be a good idea." She picked up an envelope from the small table by the door. "I've got to rush now, Mr. Everett. I just came by for this." She flashed her unopened phone bill as she walked past him into the hall. She quickly shoved the envelope into her shoulder bag and looked back at the men. "I've really got to run."

Mr. Everett held the door for the two men, closed her door, made sure it was locked, and handed her the keys. He walked along beside her toward the outside door. "I'll take care of that lock this afternoon, Miss Hale." He held the outside door for her. "I'll leave you new keys in your mailbox."

Peggy stepped outside. "Thank you, Mr. Everett. I've really got to run now. Good-bye, gentlemen," she said to them all as she ran to her car, got in, and drove out the driveway at a speed she'd never attempted before. It was a good twenty minutes before her heart stopped racing and her hands stopped shaking. She tried to determine if she was being followed, but couldn't tell. The farther east she traveled the lighter the traffic became, and that was both a blessing and a worry. With fewer cars on the wide freeway, driving was less of a strain, but she also realized she would be easier to spot, if indeed she was being followed.

The clouds became grayer the farther east she traveled. Ahead of her, the sky looked ominous. She became comfortable with the feeling that her visitors had not guessed where she was going and were not following her. Those two men had to be the ones who had been following her and Nick in the big black Ford, she decided. She had glimpsed a car like theirs when she made her fast exit from the parking lot. Who were they? Now she had more news for the lieutenant.

She had the sinking feeling she should have tried to find Nick. He had said he had a couple of errands to do but he would be at his apartment most of the time until he called her at three. He was so very different from anyone she knew. At least as far as she was concerned, last night had indeed been the start of something very big for her.

Maybe she shouldn't have been so secretive with him this morning, she thought. Maybe she should have told him what she had in mind to do with the three names she had. Maybe she should have asked him to go with her when she met with Tom Wylie. She squinted at the road. Maybe he, too, would have given her a bad time about contacting the men and would have reminded her that the lieutenant had told her not to do anything on her own. Maybe Tom Wylie wouldn't have given her the information about Mr. Tyler's blackmailing business if Nick had been along. Maybe. . . . She looked up at the dark sky and told herself that just maybe she was getting close to the edge over this whole thing.

Lieutenant Watson had not returned to the office when Peggy arrived. He had called in and, after receiving her message, left word for her to wait for him. Peggy looked at the clock on the wall. "If the lieutenant gets here before I get back, tell him I'll be back shortly. I just want to go out to the Tyler cabin and look around." She left hurriedly before the woman behind the desk could give her an argument.

She drove directly to the cabin. Although the sheriff's department had been over the place with a fine-tooth comb, she still felt there should be something there that could answer the mounting questions. She had no idea what she was looking for or what questions she expected to find answered. She did, however, have a very strong feeling she should go to the cabin alone and just look.

Peggy shivered when she got out of her car. It was more than the cold air that the sudden strong breeze generated. The gloomy sky threatened to release a storm at any minute, and everything looked desolate. She shivered again and slowly made her way around to the side of the house in shoes not really up to the task. The branch of a tree hit the side of the cabin and she jumped. She straightened her shoulders, trying to renew her courage, and that helped minimally. Just as she rounded the corner to the back of the cabin, a gloved hand clamped tightly, and none too gently, over her mouth.

She wrestled her body around and kicked as the man behind her clamped his arm around her waist and maneuvered her around to the back of the house. She tried to scream, but the sound was lost in his gloved hand. She jabbed him with her elbows and tried to attack his foot with the heel of her shoe. He groaned a couple of times, but he kept moving her forward through the trees. She lost all sense of direction as the man continued to move her forward for what seemed an endless length of time.

The sound of someone moving through the underbrush to her left caught her attention, but she couldn't see anyone. And then before them was a tall gray run-down shed Peggy hadn't seen before. The man holding her stopped and turned her to face away from the building for just a moment, until someone opened the door. Peggy took advantage of that moment by raising one leg and bringing her high heel down on the instep of the man's foot. He swore and roughly pushed her inside the shed. The door slammed shut. There was the sound of something banging against the door, footsteps leaving the building, and then silence.

Peggy had fallen to the floor with her less-than-graceful entrance to the small building. She rolled to her side and could see nothing but darkness for a minute. She sat up and looked around. Ever so slowly, she began to make out the outline of a few crates, a chainsaw, two dirty windows, and a big skylight. Then a scream caught in her throat. Not five feet from where she sat, a man's leg stuck out between two crates.

Using slow motions, as though not to disturb anyone, she stood up. Her heart raced, she had difficulty breathing, and swallowing was nearly an impossibility. With much reluctance and using extreme caution, she made her way toward the inert body that lay sprawled between two large wooden crates. She sucked in her breath and stopped short for just a moment before she reached down and touched the shoulder of Stan Tyler.

Stan groaned but didn't move. She touched him again. "Mr. Tyler, are you all right?" She bit her lip. That was a dumb question, she told herself. If he was all right, he wouldn't be lying there on the floor. She touched his shoulder again and he groaned again. He moved his head just a bit and looked up at her. She felt better seeing his eyes open. "Don't move, Mr. Tyler. If I can figure out how, I'll get out of here and get help." He put his hand up to her, but it dropped to the floor again.

Peggy stood up and ran over to the door. She shook it, banged on it, and yelled at the top of her lungs. None of her efforts netted results. She stopped and listened intently, hoping to hear some sign of life from outside, but the world was deadly quiet. She walked back to Stan, trying to think of something, anything, she could do to get out of there.

She looked up at the dirty windows. They were at least six or seven feet above her head. She pushed on one of the low wide crates, but it was so heavy she could barely move it. She tried several more, but they, too, refused to budge more than a few inches. Two or three would have to be stacked on top of one another for her to be able to get to one of the windows.

She went back to Stan and touched his shoulder again. He moved, and his eyes opened. "Mr. Tyler, can you talk to me?" She needed to know he was conscious.

He moaned. "Just give me a minute," he said, his words coming slowly. "I think I'm all right. Can you help me up?" He was trying to push himself up. Peggy got behind him and bent down. She pushed on his shoulders until he was in a sitting position.

He looked up at her and tried to smile. "Thanks, Peggy. I think I'll be okay in a minute." He rubbed his head, then looked up at her and frowned. "What happened to you? You're covered with dirt and. . . ."

She looked down at herself. Wet dirt hung from her jacket and skirt, along with an array of pine needles. She glanced at the floor. It was covered with damp footprints filled with pine needles. She ran her hand over her hair, which felt as though it had gone wild. "Someone grabbed me and then threw me in here, locked the door, and left. I didn't get a look at his face. What happened to you?"

He shook his head, then grabbed it. "I shouldn't do that. I'm not sure what happened. I was just looking around the outside of the cabin, and somebody came up behind me and zapped me a good one. I had no idea anyone was around. Did you see anyone when you arrived?"

Peggy shook her head and stood up. "No, I didn't. Where's your car, Mr. Tyler?"

He struggled to get to his feet. Peggy helped him. He closed his eyes for a moment and then opened them. "Please, call me Stan. We seem to be in the same lifeboat, so to speak. My car is parked out on the main road." He took a deep breath. "I thought someone might be here. I don't even know why I came up here, if you want to know the truth. I had a big row with Jennifer this morning and I went out, got into my rented car, and started driving. Since I don't know San Diego very well," he said with a shrug, "I came up here. If Scott had been there, I think I'd have suggested we leave. He was meeting some friends for breakfast." He rubbed his head again and weaved a little.

Peggy moved debris from the tallest of the crates. "You'd better sit down, Stan, before you fall down."

He did as he was told. "You know, Peggy, I think I've been had. I'm a fifty-two-year-old man, and I've been used like an innocent schoolboy."

Peggy looked at the gash on the back of his head. "You were sure hit a good one. You need to see a doctor." Even in the dim light, blood showed on his fair hair. She blotted his wound with a tissue from her shoulder bag.

"I don't think I need a doctor, but I do need a lot of answers."

Peggy sat down across from him on another crate. "Don't we all."

"I'd better talk to that lieutenant up here." He looked up at Peggy and tried valiantly to smile.

"That might be a marvelous idea, but we're prisoners in this badly furnished hotel. I don't even know where we are. I don't remember seeing this little building, but it can't be far from the cabin."

"I think this building is on the property next to Fred's, among some trees and hardly noticeable. I saw one about this size when I walked to the cabin from the main road." He looked around. "Maybe, when I recover a little more, we can stack these crates up and I can get to one of these windows."

Peggy nodded. "It's worth a try, but I've already found out these crates are heavy."

"You know, I was almost convinced I was inadvertently involved in the death of my brother. Along with a couple of other things I've picked up on, this crack on the head tells me I just may not be as involved as I thought."

Peggy bit her lip. Considering the situation they were in, she felt she could probably trust him. "Maybe if we exchange information, we can come up with something useful. Why don't you lean back against the wall and tell me what you know about this whole mess? Then I'll tell you everything I know that I didn't tell you yesterday at my apartment and some things I've learned since."

He nodded and winced. "I wish I wouldn't do that." He closed his eyes for a second. "Okay, I'll tell you everything I know. First, you should know that although Fred and I had nothing to do with each other, I know Jennifer quite well." From his expression Peggy got the idea it was not something he was pleased about at the moment.

She tried to smile. "I guessed that might be so."

"It's not what you may think. My wife died five years ago and, well, I've never gotten back into relationships with women. Jennifer used to come up to LA quite often just for the day. What she really wanted, I used to think, was someone to talk to. From what she told me, she and Fred were married for the public view only. They led their private lives separately." He pursed his lips. "I don't understand a marriage like that, but I know they exist."

"I've learned a little about their lives too, but do go on." She tried to get comfortable on the hard crate.

"Well, I thought I knew her quite well. I'll try to be brief, but I want you to know how I got involved in all this. I'm still not sure what I'm involved in. About a year ago, Jennifer found out that Fred was involved in something besides advertising. Although she felt it was very lucrative she couldn't figure out what it was. She found a bankbook in his desk at home that had over eighty thousand dollars in it, and the account was in his name only. They had a big blowup about it. He said it was money he'd held out of the advertising firm to start a separate PR business. She said the bankbook was gone the next day." He grinned. "She'd had a key made to his desk after telling a locksmith she'd lost the key."

"Clever," Peggy said. She jumped up and walked across the room and picked up a crowbar. "I just spotted this. While we talk, we might see what's in these crates that makes them so heavy. We'll never be able to stack them as they are."

He stood up and took the crowbar from her and went to work on one of the crates while he continued. "Anyway, she had told me they were going to San Francisco Tuesday for a little holiday to try to straighten out their lives. Monday night, Fred told her to go on alone and do some shopping and he'd join her Wednesday. He said he had a toothache and their dentist said he'd work Fred in the next day. She went to the airport Tuesday, but she didn't leave. He didn't go home Tuesday night, and she was furious. When he came home Wednesday night, she just said she'd decided not to go. She called me Thursday with that story."

"It won't look good for her that she's lied about that San Francisco trip." Peggy watched him struggle with the crowbar. She could hardly wait to hear the rest of his story.

"She called me Friday noon in hysterics. I could hardly understand her. That morning, she had found an airline ticket to Greece for the next day in his jacket pocket while he was in the shower. She asked him about it, and he said the airline had made a mistake. It was supposed to be for two, and the airline was taking care of it. It was supposed to be a surprise for her, he said. He told her to meet him at the cabin up here at eight that night and he'd explain everything. He had to meet a man up here to settle a deal. He said they could go away on a second honeymoon. He told her he had over a million dollars now and they had it made." He paused and rubbed his head.

"Stan, are you all right?" She walked over and looked at his wound. She touched it lightly. "It's stopped bleeding, I think."

"I just have a monumental headache. Anyway, Jennifer didn't buy his story about the airline's making a mistake, and she didn't want a honeymoon. She was afraid he'd get violent when she told him. They both left the house at nine Friday morning. When she returned home, his car was there but he wasn't. She looked in the wall safe, and all their stocks and bonds were gone. She called their bank, and their savings account had been closed. She disguised her voice and learned that your office still thought he was in San Francisco. Jennifer was sure he'd come up to the cabin. She wanted me to come down to San Diego and face Fred with her. She said she was afraid of Fred physically. She'd told me that before. I knew he had a bad temper."

Peggy frowned. "Some of that information fits with what I learned from Tom Wylie and Leslie Adams."

"Who are they?"

"You'll find out when we get to my story." She took the crowbar from his hand. "Sit down," she ordered. "You're weaving. You have that nearly open, so I should be able to finish it. Did you come up here with her?"

He cleared his throat. "My first mistake was to believe everything she told me. My second was to believe her hysterics. Jennifer can be very charismatic. Be very leery of charismatic people, Peggy."

She raised her eyebrows. "I'll remember that."

"Anyway, after her frantic call, Scott and I dropped everything and caught the next plane to San Diego. Scott has some friends down there he's been intending to visit. Jennifer and I arrived at the cabin before five. Fred was ready to walk out the door when we opened it and walked in. After he recovered from the shock of seeing us, he flew into a rage because I was there. Then he and Jennifer launched into a verbal battle such as I've never witnessed and hope never to witness again. My wife claimed I didn't have the instincts of a good fighter, but that I could do battle with just a look." He smiled and looked at Peggy directly for the first time. "It isn't anything I do on purpose, but I guess I can be intimidating without knowing it. I'm not a violent man, I assure you." He cleared his throat.

Peggy believed him. Her first impression was that he was a shy man. She had been correct. Nick hadn't thought so. It was his eyes, she was sure. They had bothered her at first too. She wondered about Nick. Had he called the office at three as she'd told him to? Was he on his way up there? Would he find them? What about the lieutenant? She clenched her teeth and gave the crowbar a good push. "You couldn't have messed up the cabin then, because the sheriff's deputies would have noticed it when they flashed their lights inside," she said breathlessly.

"No, I don't know when that happened. Anyway, Jennifer knew more about Fred than he thought she did. I couldn't believe it when she called him a blackmailer. Going through his desk on a regular basis, she learned about a condo he had. She had told one of the maintenance men she'd left her keys at her friend's house and showed him ID that proved she was Mrs. Fred Tyler, and he let her into the condo. There she'd found all kinds of information that told her about her husband's other business. She'd been waiting for the right time to use it to blackmail him, but seeing that airline ticket apparently made her feel the time was right. Anyway, she figured he had a good sum of money stashed somewhere, and she wanted her share. He laughed at her. It all came as a big surprise to me."

Peggy gave one good push on the crowbar, and the top of the crate popped up. In it was an outboard engine. "I'll try another. You sit still. Go on. I can't wait to hear what happened next."

"I hate having you do that, but I know I'm not much help. Anyway, Fred gave her a good push over the back of the couch. Then he pushed me. As I said, I'm not a violent man, but I was pretty much undone by all I'd heard. I pushed him back and we went at it back and forth for a few minutes, like a pair of kids. He fell backward to the floor and couldn't get up. One leg was twisted behind him. He winced at first and then he laughed. 'You'll never find the money, Jen,' he said. Then I had a real shock. She took a big gun from her bag and aimed it at him. 'I think you'll tell me,' she said very calmly.

"I was nearly paralyzed by the scene before me. Fred stuttered and stammered for a minute, and then she cocked that gun and stepped closer to him. He yelled at her, told her about a floor safe at the condo, and rattled off the combination. She went to the desk and scribbled the number down. She turned back to him, aiming the gun at him again. 'You'd better be telling the truth,' she said in a voice I don't think he doubted. He swore he was."

"Did she shoot him then?"

"No. I was afraid she might, but she sat down on the couch and asked him about the two hundred fifty thousand dollars for Tom Wylie. She wanted to know if that was in the safe too. Fred's face dropped, and when he didn't answer, she told him that she'd found a note in a wastebasket at his condo. The note had referred to the money and to meeting Wylie at the cabin with it.

"Fred's mouth fell open. It took him a minute to think of an answer, I guess. He never took his eyes from her gun. It was a tense moment. Finally he said that he was supposed to meet Wylie at the cabin at nine. That the money was in an attaché case in the office safe. She laughed and reminded him he was ready to leave when we arrived. He said she could call Wylie and check. He'd planned to go to San Diego, get his own money from his condo safe, and return to the cabin to meet her at eight. Together they'd wait for Wylie. In the meantime, he said he'd called you to bring the case with the money for Wylie up to the cabin so he wouldn't have to go to the office, since everyone thought he was in San Francisco. He said he didn't want to get hung up with business."

"Didn't that sound flaky to you?"

"I wasn't too alert. I didn't try to examine it for credibility. All I wanted to do was to get Jennifer out of there."

Peggy struggled with the corner of a crate. She

couldn't get the crowbar to budge. Stan stood up and helped her. They both used all their weight to pry the top open; when it gave, the crowbar slipped and knocked Stan to the floor. Peggy dropped beside him. "Stan, are you okay?"

He struggled to a sitting position. He moved his right arm and looked up at her. "I think I've damaged my arm now, Peg. I guess you're on your own." She helped him stand up.

After she got him seated again, she went back to the crate and picked up the crowbar. "That should be my only problem. Tell me more of this fascinating story. It sounds like a movie script to me."

Stan leaned back against the wall. "When I got my wits together, I tried to grab the gun from Jennifer. She yanked it back, ran over to Fred, and hit him briskly on the front of his head with the gun butt. He put his hand to his forehead and fell backward against a chair. Then she handed me the gun. We locked the door and left. I knew right then I was in over my head.

"She drove down the road to the grocery store. She stopped and called your apartment. When you didn't answer, she called your office. Fred's secretary told her you had left for the cabin with an attaché case. Then she called Tom Wylie and asked him if he had an appointment with her husband at the cabin. Tom said yes, but he wasn't going to get there at nine. He said it would probably be closer to eleven. She seemed satisfied.

"When she started the car, she suddenly realized she'd dropped her brooch and a scarf. She said the brooch was very valuable and insisted we go back for it. By then I was numb. She parked out on the main road, and we walked back through the woods. We saw your car. The house was dark. Jennifer got in your car and was about to check the registration when we saw you. She didn't recognize you in that light. We didn't know whose car it was until you arrived the next morning."

"You shot at me!"

He leaned down and put his elbows on his knees, his head in his hands. "Yes, but, believe me, it was a ploy born of desperation. I'm a good shot. I didn't aim to hit you. I only wanted to scare you off until we could get out of there."

"You did a good job."

"We ran down the road faster than you ran into the woods."

"Were you driving your brother's silver Porsche?"

"Yes. Jennifer had managed to get duplicates of all of Fred's keys. I don't know how I got into all this."

"I can understand that feeling. Did she get her brooch and her scarf?"

"No, by the time we saw you, I'd had more than enough. I ran down the road and she came after me."

Another crate opened. It contained an engine

labeled *Power Generator.* Peggy laid down the crowbar. "We should find something to give us a little light." In a corner, she found an old rusty kerosene lamp. "Shall we see if this works?" She brought it over to him.

Stan shook it. "There's some fuel still left in it." He struck a match to the wick and the room lit up. He moved the lantern to the crate beside him and smiled. She returned his smile, seeing him now as a rather pathetic figure. "Then what did you do?" A lot of her questions had been answered, but not all. If Jennifer Tyler hit her husband on the front of his head, what about the bloody gash on the back of his head that Nick saw in the photos? She went to work on another crate.

Stan lit a cigarette. "We went to the condo, and I found a new meaning for the word *fury.*"

Peggy gave Stan her undivided attention. "What happened?"

"The first thing Jennifer did was open the safe. There was the million dollars in it, all right. I knew why Fred laughed. It was in the form of ten one hundred thousand dollar gold certificates on a Swiss bank. To Jennifer, they were useless." He rubbed his neck. "Jennifer went into a rage the likes of which I've never seen. She threw lamps, tipped over furniture, threw dishes, and in general destroyed or at least upset everything she could get her hands on in that condo. I tried to stop her but had things thrown at me for my effort. When she calmed down, she started to cry. She apologized for throwing things at me and for all the rest of her actions."

Peggy shivered. She was getting cold again. Even though she had decided it was probably futile, she went to work on yet another crate.

"By that time, my neck and shoulders were paining me unmercifully from my struggle with Fred. Jennifer dropped me at the nearest emergency room and told me to call Scott to pick me up. She had an errand to do. At the hospital, they X-rayed my neck and my shoulders, told me nothing was terminal, gave me some pain pills and this neck brace, and told me to take it easy.

"Scott was out with friends that night. I've hardly seen him since we arrived in San Diego. He has a lot of friends down there. Anyway, I called a cab and went back to Jennifer's house. I took a pain pill as soon as I got there and promptly fell asleep. Scott woke me about four-thirty, and he said Jennifer had awakened him and told him about the call from the sheriff. She told him she wanted me to get up to the cabin between seven-thirty and eight o'clock and to say I'd just arrived from LA. Scott didn't understand it. I understood it, but I didn't like it."

"How much does Scott know?"

"I haven't told Scott any of this. I told him, as I told them at the hospital, that I'd fallen from a ladder at the cabin."

Peggy pried a top off one of the smaller crates.

"Olé!" she said. The box was filled with smaller boxes, each one heavy for its size but easy enough to lift out. "We can empty this crate and maybe get it onto one of the higher ones. I hope there are a few more crates with this kind of stuff. I hate to think what the man who owns these things will think when he sees this mess."

Stan started lifting boxes from the crate. Peggy could see it was painful for him. "I'll do it," she said.

"I should do something here," he said with a bashful smile. "I plan to have Scott come back and help me straighten up whatever mess we may make. I think these small boxes have engine parts in them. Whoever owns all this must be a mechanic of some sort."

"At least he's a collector," Peggy said. After emptying the crate with much effort, they managed to get the empty crate on top of another crate. The stacked crates weren't high enough for either of them to reach the window. They sat down to catch their breath. Peggy took the opportunity to ask a question. "Do you know anything about two men who've been calling me about the two hundred fifty thousand dollars and following me?"

He closed his eyes for a moment. "Jennifer hired them. She gave them specific instructions on just how she wanted you harassed about the money. She thought you might have it or know something about it. She insisted that they imitate

Fred's voice. She thought it would unnerve you. I heard only the last part of her conversation. I think she has some flaky friends."

Peggy pursed her lips. "They unnerved me all right." She told him about their being at her apartment that day and about the other man who had been following her. "I guess she thought there'd be safety in numbers."

"I know one thing," Stan said as he stood up and moved his shoulders gently, "I'm going to reevaluate my whole manner of reading people. I really thought I knew Jennifer. Today I can tell you I didn't know her at all. It's hard to believe I was so wrong about her." He shrugged. "One is never too old to learn, I guess. If you don't have any more questions for me, what have you learned that I don't know about?"

Peggy went to work on another crate and told him almost everything she knew. She hoped she was right in her evaluation of him. She saw him as one who was as inadvertently caught in this mess as she was herself. His biggest crime was to lie to the police.

"You know, there are things still not accounted for," she said. "Mr. Kolby said another car came a few minutes after I left. I know that was Leslie's. I know the car that came late and left quickly was Tom Wylie's. What we don't know is who was in the car that came and stayed awhile between Leslie and Tom Wylie. I bet it was Jennifer. Mr. Wylie saw the silver Porsche and thought it was your brother's. I suppose you have no idea what time Jennifer came home that night after she left you at the hospital."

"No, I went right to sleep. Scott said he got home about one o'clock and she wasn't home then."

Peggy digested that as another crate lid came loose. That crate was filled with small boxes of nuts and bolts and small parts. She started talking as she pulled the boxes out of the crate. "You said Jennifer hit your brother on the front of the head and, as far as you know, he was alive when you left."

Stan stood up to help her. "Yes, I'm sure he was. I think at most he may have been stunned or dazed for a while. It didn't appear she hit him hard. Of course, I'm no expert on the subject."

She stood beside the empty box and looked at him. "One thing I didn't tell you was that your brother died from a blow on the head. However, Nick saw the pictures, and he said the gash was on the back of his head."

With more strength than Peggy knew she had, she helped Stan manipulate the empty crate to the top of the other two they had stacked. Again, they both sat down to get their breath back. Stan laughed lightly. "You can probably tell that even without my shoulders and neck and arm being injured I'm not an overly physical man."

"I'm not much into physical things, either," Peggy said dryly. "What time do you have?"

He looked at his watch. "It's almost five o'clock. It's pretty dark out there now."

She nodded. "You're right. I wonder if Nick is here yet. I left word for him that I was coming up, and the lieutenant at the sheriff's office knows I went out to the cabin. They both should be looking for me by now." She looked over at the lantern. "You know, I've always taken a great deal of pride in the fact that I could take care of my own problems, that I wasn't a dependent woman who had to have someone taking care of things for me, that I could bloody well go it alone. You may have learned you're not always great at judging people, but I've learned it may not be so dumb to ask for help once in a while. It's always possible that someone else might have a better idea than I have, I guess."

Stan smiled. "Don't beat up on yourself."

"Well, I shouldn't have come here alone."

"The evidence suggests I shouldn't have, either."

Peggy smiled at him for his compassion. "I should have called Nick."

"He's pretty important to you, huh?"

"Yes, he is. It feels a little funny. I've never been one much for dating. I've listened to my friends talk about it and at times it's seemed a lot more work than pleasure. My mother says it's because I haven't met many men who appeal to me. She always said that when I did fall, I'd fall hard and fast. I may have done that with Nick even though I haven't known him long. I hope I know what I'm doing." She made a face. "I may never see him again, but if I do, I'm sure he's going to be furious at me for coming up here alone."

"I'm sure he will be. Steel yourself for his fury. You'll see him again."

She jumped up, a little embarrassed for baring her soul to this man, yet feeling better for having done it. She looked down at him. "Shall we see what we can do to get out of this haven in the trees?" She walked over to the stack of crates. "I think I'm going to appreciate the concrete jungle and the palm trees a lot more after this experience in the country."

He stood up slowly and grinned. "Me too. Let me see what we have here. I've got to figure a way to get up to the top of our mountain of crates."

Peggy took off her high heels and pulled up her skirt. "If you'll boost me up to the first crate here, I think I can get to that second one and then on top of our pile. I sure wish I'd changed to jeans and running shoes. This would be a lot easier."

"From what you said, you hardly had a chance. You'd better let me try it, Peggy. I'd hate to have you fall. You'll never get down to the ground from that window without hurting yourself."

"Your neck and shoulders and arm would limit your agility. Also, I don't plan to have to get down from that window. Considering the time, I'm willing to bet that Nick is at the cabin and looking around the area for me. With my car still there, I feel sure he and the sheriff's department are combing the woods. I plan to break a window up there and start yelling. My father used to say I was born with the strongest pair of lungs of any kid on the block. Let's hope they're still in good form. Come on, give me a boost."

Stan did not agree with her fully, but he did as he was asked. With more than a little difficulty, she made it to the top. Stan threw one of her shoes up to her, and she used it to break a window. Then she started yelling. She called Nick's name and she yelled for help several times in a row before she stopped to rest.

"Your father was right, you know," Stan said. "You do have a good pair of lungs."

"I'm glad they're still working. I haven't used them to this extent for some time." She started yelling again, and then she rested.

During her fourth rest, she heard a distant response. "Miss Hale, is that you?"

When the door to the shed was opened, Nick was the first one inside, followed by three deputies and Lieutenant Watson. Nick grabbed Peggy and held her tightly, burying his face in her neck for a minute. Then he pulled back and gazed at her. "Why didn't you call me before you came up here?" he asked in the tone an irate father would use with his errant child.

Anger started to rise in Peggy, but it quickly subsided as she looked up at his face. She threw herself against him and embraced him tightly. "Because I'm all the dumb things you're thinking I am." She looked over his shoulder and saw the lieutenant smiling at them.

Back at the station house, Stan told the lieutenant everything he had told Peggy. She, in turn, told the lieutenant everything she'd learned that day. The lieutenant listened to her, his expression stern. "I should be angry at you." He took a deep breath and leaned forward. "We've learned something, also. Everything we can find with Fred Tyler's name on it is mortgaged to the hilt, including his half of the Tyler Advertising Agency." He picked up the phone and called Sergeant Burke in San Diego. He told him everything, listened a few minutes, said thanks, and hung up. "They'll pick up Mrs. Tyler for questioning."

Nick, who had been listening intently, looked around at everyone and squeezed Peggy's hand. "It looks to me as though Fred Tyler had everything well planned. He was going to skip out on everyone. He was ready to leave the cabin when Stan and Jennifer arrived around five. If Tyler had left then, that would leave Leslie with her suitcases when she arrived at six. Peggy would have arrived at the dark cabin at seven, Jennifer would have been left waiting alone at eight, and

Wylie would have been left with an attaché case full of newspapers. Randall Barker, of course, would be left with a business loaded with debts."

The lieutenant leaned back in his chair. "Fred Tyler's scheme wasn't as perfect as he thought. Tom Wylie talked to Sergeant Burke this afternoon as he promised Peggy he'd do. His payoff was to be two hundred fifty thousand dollars. Tyler told him he could watch the office building that housed Tyler Advertising around four and he'd see Peggy leaving with the attaché case. He assured Wylie that his papers and some of his money would be in that case. Tyler expected to get the rest of Wylie's money from Castleberry Friday afternoon at the cabin. If Castleberry was there, I guess Mr. Kolby across the way missed seeing his car." He stood up. "You can ride down to San Diego with me, Mr. Tyler. They want to talk to you too. I'll have someone take care of your car."

Peggy stood up. "If someone will take me to my car, I'll meet you all at the station."

Nick grabbed her arm. "I'll take you," he said gruffly. "I have a long list of things I want to say to you."

Peggy made a face. "Oh, I'm sure you have."

By the time they all arrived at the San Diego police station, Sergeant Burke had already been to the Tyler house, but he had found no one home. "The house was dark and there was no one around. I have two men out there waiting for Mrs. Tyler to come home."

Peggy thought a minute, then asked Stan, "Do you have a key to the house?"

"Yes. Jennifer gave me one when I arrived. Why?"

"I guess the police can't use it, but we could go out there, couldn't we? It's possible she's just not answering the door and is sitting in the dark. At the very least, we might be able to find that gun and maybe some other things that could help."

Lieutenant Watson was the first to say, "Now, Peggy. . . ."

Sergeant Burke frowned. "Miss Hale, you could get hurt. This is police business. You—"

"Sergeant," Peggy interrupted him, "is Stan Tyler under arrest?"

The sergeant frowned. "No, but we need a statement from him."

"There's no reason he couldn't give me his key, is there?"

"Miss Hale—"

She cut him off. "Look, you said you have two men out there. Maybe Nick and I can go into the house and find something to tell us where she might be. Tom Wylie said he thought Fred Tyler and Randall Barker were there at the cabin because he saw both their Porsches. We know Jennifer Tyler was driving that silver Porsche that night. She drove Stan up there in it. She's got to be the one who was there when Tom Wylie arrived around ten-thirty. What we don't know is who was with her. I can't imagine who that might have been. The lieutenant told me Mr. Tyler was badly beaten. Stan didn't beat him up, he only pushed him and he fell, apparently breaking his leg. Jennifer couldn't have done it alone. Maybe we can find something helpful. If we run into any problem, sergeant, we can let your guys know."

"No, Peggy." Lieutenant Watson was sounding like her father again.

Stan tried to hold back a smile as he pulled the key from his pocket. The sergeant let out an exasperated breath. "Okay, we'll all go." He glared at Peggy. "This time, you do exactly as you're told. Do you understand?"

"Yes, sir," she said demurely.

The Tyler house sat back from the street in an area of other large white stucco homes built for elegance years ago. Each wide front yard was professionally landscaped and neatly maintained. The driveways were long, and most were lined with palm trees, oleanders, or hibiscus. The Tyler house had oleanders that were tall and full and partially concealed it. When they arrived, Peggy told Nick to park in front and turn out his lights. The police cars that followed them—with the lieutenant, the sergeant, and three uniformed men—did the same. They all met on the side-walk.

Peggy spoke first. "I think if Stan and I go in and Jennifer happens to be there, the shock will—"

Sergeant Burke did not agree. "Miss Hale, I will not allow you to—"

But she didn't let him finish. "Look, sergeant, whoever grabbed me today turned me aside while someone opened the door to that shed. I've been thinking about that. It was not a big person, not the size of an average man, and this person was very light on his or her feet. I'd bet anything it was Jennifer Tyler. If she should be in there, I'd like to see her face when she sees us. You just stay far enough away so she won't see you. Believe me, I'm no hero. I think Stan and I may be able to get more out of her. If she sees you, she'll clam up and yell for her lawyer. You remember how she was at the office?"

Lieutenant Watson, who didn't really have jurisdiction in the city, was totally against the idea. Sergeant Burke wasn't thrilled with it, but he could see its merits. "I'll let you do it against my better judgment, Miss Hale, but you'll do it my way."

"You got it," she said.

The sergeant sent his men up the side of the property. They crouched down and went around the house to cover the back door and the two side entrances Stan told them about. The lieutenant and the sergeant also moved up the side of the property and stationed themselves just beside the wide porch as close to the front door as they could get. Nick followed and stationed himself alongside the house, promising to stay out of the way.

When everyone was in position, Stan and Peggy walked up the long driveway. Stan inserted the key into the door, pushed it open, and stepped into the foyer. He flipped on the light. Peggy stepped in behind him, being careful not to close the door completely. The house was quiet and almost dark. A dim light came from the rear. Peggy held her breath. In a room straight ahead of them sat five big pieces of matched luggage.

Jennifer Tyler came from the dimly lit area, talking before she rounded the corner. "Honey, what are you doing with that light on. . . ." Her voice dropped and she stopped dead still when she saw Peggy and Stan. "What are you two. . . ." The woman became speechless.

Stan glared at her. "What are we doing here? Is that what you wanted to ask, Jennifer? You may have forgotten, I'm your houseguest."

"Hey, Jen, if you're talking to me, I can't hear you. I'm just about ready to go." The voice came from upstairs. "It hasn't been easy cleaning up by the light of a flashlight, you know."

Stan and Peggy looked at each other. They both recognized the voice.

Chapter Nine

S tan turned back to Jennifer. "We know you went back to the cabin after you left me at the hospital, Jennifer. You killed my brother."

Her mouth fell open. "I didn't kill Fred. He did. He beat Fred up. Fred was brutal, he—"

Scott Tyler came down the stairs. "Sure, I beat him up," he said. "He was violent when we arrived. His leg was broken, but he was ready to fight. But who held the gun to his head until he told us where he had the money hidden? She was certain he had a lot of cash." He glanced at Jennifer and then looked at his father. "He came at me with a knife, and I fell back against the fireplace. When he glanced at Jennifer I picked up a poker and hit him on the head. He fell to the floor. Jennifer found his briefcase hidden in the bedroom. It was filled with cash. The old boy planned to go away in style. But we thought there should be more—the two hundred fifty thousand dollars Peggy had brought earlier in the attaché case. We tore the place apart because Jennifer thought Peggy might have come back with it after she was scared off. When we couldn't find it, Jennifer went outside and shot the lock off the back door, came in, and put two bullets into her husband so it would look like someone broke in." Scott almost smiled. "I was shaking like a leaf, but let me tell you she never blinked an eye. She just looked up at me and said we could go to South America and get lost—after we got Peggy to turn over the money she had."

Stan stared at his son. "How long has this been going on with you two?"

Jennifer laughed. Scott cleared his throat and looked at her. "When she came to LA, she'd have dinner with you and then she'd meet me. I'm sorry, Dad, but, well, it just happened. I'm a big boy now, you know."

Stan nodded. "It always just happens." He looked at Jennifer. "You've taken to younger men."

She squared her shoulders. "I like younger men. Older men are bores."

Stan glared at his son. "You zapped me on the head?"

"Sorry, Dad. We didn't want you to see us. Jennifer knew Peggy was on her way up there, and it worried her. Some guys who had been following Peggy called. They got stopped by an accident, but they'd seen Peggy turn east on Highway 8. We finally realized that Peggy wasn't holding out on us, that there probably never was two hundred fifty thousand dollars set aside for Wylie in that case she had carried. But she has a big nose problem. We were afraid she had found out too much, and we knew we'd better cut our losses and run, which is what we're about to do. I'm afraid we're going to have to zap you again so we can get out of here."

Stan reached behind him and opened the door. "Come in, sergeant," he said. The sergeant and the lieutenant stepped in the door.

Scott looked at his father. "Dad, get me a lawyer."

Stan Tyler's cold green eyes bore into his son. "Get your own lawyer, Scott. You're a big boy now."

Nick followed Peggy back to her apartment. "I want to talk to you," he said firmly as soon as he closed the door.

"Look, if you're going to bawl me out, forget it. I'm not up to it tonight. I know I was stupid to go up there alone, but it's over and done with, thank goodness."

He pulled her into his arms. "That's not what I want to talk to you about." He covered her lips with his and held her close.

When he raised his head, she swallowed and said, "I like this talk."

He dropped his arms and held her away from him. "I was worried to death about you today. I almost went crazy when I found your car and couldn't find you. By the way, you look a mess."

"Thanks."

He squeezed her hands. "My friends have told

me that when I met the right woman, the woman I'd love for the rest of my life, I'd know it right away. It's taken so long that some said it would happen fast when the time finally came. I used to laugh, but now I know they were right. If I didn't love you so much, I still would have been worried about you when you were missing, but I wouldn't have gone half crazy when you couldn't be found. What we have to talk about is how long we should wait before we tell our parents, so they won't have coronaries. After that, we can spend the rest of our lives together smiling every time it rains."

"I think we should celebrate rain."

"Sounds good to me." He pulled her back into his arms and kissed her, a kiss they both knew had been worth waiting for.